A Desperate
Search

© Day One Publications 2014

First printed 2014

✦   ISBN 978-1-84625-428-4

All Scripture quotations are based on the **New International Version** 1984 Copyright © 1973, 1978, 1984

Published by Day One Publications
Ryelands Road, Leominster, HR6 8NZ

TEL 01568 613 740 FAX 01568 611 473

email—sales@dayone.co.uk

UK web site—www.dayone.co.uk

Designed by **documen**
Printed by TJ International

Dedication

This book is dedicated to my grandsons—
Jacob and Dylan, born during the writing
of this book.

MACEDONIA

Neapolis
Philippi

GALATIA

PAMPHYLIA

Perga
Lystra

Antioch
Seleucia

SYRIA

CYPRUS
Paphos

Caesarea
Jerusalem

JUDEA

100 mi
200 km

ALEX AND MATT'S JOURNEYS

4

Chapter one

"**A**lexander!"

The boy paused for a moment before heaving the javelin with all his might across the yard where his friend was standing.

"Not bad, Alex!" Mattias shouted, "A metre further than your last throw."

Alex laughed, punching the air with his fist. "Olympics, here I come!"

His friend grinned, "You've got to get into the Antioch games first," he said.

"Alexander!" The voice was louder this time and more urgent.

"That's your mother calling you Alex," Matt said.

"Yes, I know," Alex replied, "We'd better go back I suppose."

Reluctantly, the two friends left their game and walked slowly towards the house. They were so very different. Alex, tall and athletic, with a face that looked as if at any moment it would break into a smile and his friend short and dark and serious.

Sophia was standing at the door waiting for them. Her hands were clasped together, and she wore a worried look on her face.

"What's up?" Alex asked as he reached her.

"It's Irana," his mother sighed, "she's been out all day and I'm anxious about her."

Matt looked worried, "Where will we find her?" he asked.

"She'll be down at Agatha's house I expect," Alex replied in disgust, "I don't know what she sees in that old witch."

"Please go and bring her home, Alexander, I don't like her being there so often."

Agatha lived in the centre of town and as they walked towards her home Alex and Matt were silent for a while. They were both thinking about Alex's sister. Irana was 13 now; a year older than the boys. Matt admired her very much although he had never admitted it to his friend. Everyone agreed there was something very special about Irana. Since she was a young girl she had been different from other children. Her bright flaming red hair made her stand out from other girls. She also had a kind of sixth sense and seemed to be able to tell the future. People believed that the gods had given this power to her.

Two things had changed though, in the past year. First of all, Irana had got to know Agatha, an old woman who was a priestess of the Egyptian goddess Isis. Agatha claimed to have special power from Isis, to heal the sick and to interpret people's dreams. There was nothing unusual about this, as Antioch was full of different gods and priests claiming to have special powers. People were very concerned not to make these gods angry and made offerings of food at their shrines. Even Alex's own family had regularly gone to the temple of Zeus until a few months ago.

But that was the other thing that had changed. A year ago some men from Cyprus had come to Antioch. They called themselves people of 'The Way' and were followers of a god called Jesus who they said had been killed and then amazingly had come alive again.

Alex's thoughts came to a sudden stop as he came in sight of Agatha's home. His sister was standing outside, talking to a large woman and an even larger man who were obviously not from Antioch. Beside them stood a cart attached to a mule. Another woman stood nearby with her back to him, but he recognised her immediately as Agatha because of her wild uncombed hair. As she turned, Alex could see she was looking very pleased with herself and he felt a cold chill of fear.

"What's going on?" Matt asked uneasily.

"I don't know," Alex replied quickening his pace, "but those people are up to no good."

"Irana!" Alex called as they drew closer, "Mother says you are to come home." The man glanced up at him and then spoke to the girl who nodded her head. Agatha turned her evil gaze on Alex. "Go back, boy," she croaked, "Tell your mother she's not coming."

Alex moved quickly towards the group with Matt closely at his side. "Irana!" he said urgently as he got close to his sister, "You must come home with me now. These are not good people."

"Yes," Matt agreed, "Please come, Irana. You're not safe here."

Irana turned her face to her brother and friend. Her face looked different somehow. Blank. There was no expression as she looked at them, almost as if she didn't know who they were. Then she spoke. "It's alright, they are going to make me famous," she said but even her voice sounded strange, "They can see how the gods have blessed me and they will take care of me."

"No!" Alex said and caught her arm, while Matt tried to take her other arm but immediately the man hit out, punching Matt in the eye and knocking Alex to the ground with a vicious push.

"Get up and clear off before something worse happens to you!" the man snarled. Matt put out a hand to help Alex as he scrambled to his feet while his other hand covered his stinging eye. Together they saw Irana being helped onto the cart by the woman. She sat there quite calmly with a far-away look on her face.

"Irana! No!" Alex shouted pushing past the sneering Agatha as he tried to reach the mule cart, only to be kicked to the ground again by the man.

From his position on the ground Alex saw the man handing Agatha three bronze coins before climbing into the cart beside Irana. Agatha's smug smile changed into a frown as she looked at the coins. "I was promised more than this," she whined. "Be thankful you have anything, old woman," he sneered, "as I suspect she wasn't yours to sell."

The next moment Alex and Matt watched with horror, as the mule cart move off, carrying Irana away. "You wicked woman! What have you done?" Alex screamed at Agatha, but she just spat on the ground by his feet, turned and went into her house.

Chapter two

"**W**hat do you mean, gone?"

Alex was badly out of breath from his frantic dash home. His father and brother Gabriel had heard his arrival and had come out of the workshop and joined his mother in the kitchen to see what all the fuss was about.

"Alex, do stop gabbling and tell us what happened!" his father said.

"It's Agatha! She's sold Irana to people who took her away in a mule cart," Alex gasped. "We tried to stop them but they were too strong for us. Matt got punched in the eye and I got pushed over. But please, you must hurry if you want to save Irana!"

"Oh Kostas!" Alex's mother cried to her husband, "Quick! Take the horses. You should be able to catch them before they get too far."

"Come, Gabriel," Kostas said running towards the door, "And Sophia, look after the boy, he's badly shaken ... that woman will pay for this!" The next moment, Kostas and Gabriel were urging their horses into a gallop down the road towards Agatha's house.

Alex watched as his father and brother disappeared. "They will catch them," he told his mother, "They must!"

Suddenly, the shock of what had happened hit him and he collapsed onto the mat and burst into tears.

Sophia, who had also been staring down the road after her husband, turned round, "You're bleeding," she said noticing for the first time the cut on Alex's leg where the man's boot had kicked him. "Come, let me clean you up while you tell me exactly what happened." Then, as if she was glad to be doing something, she quickly bustled round finding some clean water and a bandage to dress the wound.

"What about Matt?" Sophia asked quickly, "Is he alright?"

"His eye looked very sore," Alex replied, "but he went home to see if his father could do anything and I just ran as fast as I could to get here."

Sophia said little as she heard Alex's story. Occasionally, she would make exclamations such as, "The monster!" or "Oh poor Matt!" and "How could they!" but at the end she was quiet. "If only," she said when Alex had finished, "if only we had realised Irana was getting involved in such evil. All these years we've tried to please the gods. How wrong we were. But now we know ..." Sophia took a deep breath and then said very quietly, as if to herself, "we know that there is only one true God." She paused and stood up straight. "We must take heart," she said, "for our God is great, and our God is good."

At last there was no more to be said. Alex sat silent while his mother prayed desperately that Irana would be found in time. The sounds of their cow protesting because she hadn't been milked and the complaints of the chicken in the yard waiting to be fed were ignored. It was as if, at that moment, the world stood still.

Alex leaned his exhausted body against his mother and fell into a troubled sleep.

Chapter three

A few days had passed since that dreadful day. Alex was sitting in his favourite place on the roof of the house, resting his leg which was swollen and bruised. Matt was sitting beside him. His eye was getting better but it was still black and blue where the man had punched him. From their position they had a great view of the little houses all around them, shining brilliant white in the sun. Beyond the houses was a grove of olive trees, these too were shining because of the sunshine, their leaves were green and silver. They could also see the road below and could watch the people passing with their horses and carts carrying fruit and vegetables and other items to and from the market.

"My father tried to catch them too," Matt was explaining to his friend. "He went to the highway to see if they had gone that way and then to the docks, but he couldn't see them." He sighed sadly, "What happened with your father and brother?"

Alex rubbed his hands over his eyes. His usually cheerful face was sad as he answered his friend. "They went straight to Agatha's house, but she said she knew nothing about it and that I was making up stories. Father threatened her, but she wouldn't say anything."

"What did they do then?" Matt asked.

"Well, they left Agatha's house and went straight to the temple of Zeus," Alex explained.

"Whatever did they do that for?" Matt exclaimed in disgust. "I thought you were followers of Jesus now and had stopped worshipping gods made out of wood and stone."

"No, you don't understand, Matt," Alex replied, "They weren't going to worship! Don't forget the couple who took Irana were Romans and everyone knows that Romans usually pray to Jupiter before going on a journey. Father thought he might be able to catch them there."

"I thought you said the temple of Zeus," Matt said, "Now you're talking about Jupiter."

"Zeus, Jupiter! Same god, different name," Alex said, "It all depends on whether you're Greek or Roman."

"Well, I'm Jewish and I'm confused," Matt sighed.

"Anyway, they weren't at the temple so father and Gabriel went down to the docks and spoke to one of the ship workers." Alex continued, "It seems that a mule cart and three people were seen getting onto a ship."

"And where was the ship heading?" Matt asked.

"That's the trouble," Alex replied, "There were five ships in the harbour that day and no one can remember which ship they got on to. It could have been Caesarea, Cyprus, Perga, Neapolis or even Rome!"

"Hmmm," Matt said, "that's not too helpful. She could be anywhere in the Roman Empire by now."

"I know that," Alex said turning his head away to hide the tears that had come to his eyes, "I don't want to talk about it any more."

There was silence between the two friends for a while and then Matt asked, "So what now?"

"I don't know," Alex said miserably, "Irana has disappeared. No one knows where she's been taken and unless a miracle happens we'll never see her again."

"Well, we've seen a few miracles since Barnabas and Saul have been here in Antioch," Matt said, trying to encourage his friend. "And the Church is praying for Irana, so I'm sure we'll see her again."

"That's what mum and dad think," Alex answered, "But I don't think I can sit and wait for a miracle. I've got to try to find her." Alex lifted his head as a sudden look of determination came into his eyes. He reached out his hand to his friend. "I'm going to search the whole Roman Empire until I find her. Will you help me Matt?"

Matt looked back at his friend and without hesitation he grasped the hand held out to him, "I will" he said, "Together we will find her."

Chapter four

Alex and Matt had been helping in Kostas' workshop all morning. A wealthy Roman had asked them to make four large panels to be put around the entrance of his grand home. Gabriel had already carved out patterns on two of these panels and the four men who worked for Kostas were busy painting them and decorating them with jewels.

"How are you getting on lads?" Gabriel asked, putting his hammer and chisel down to come over to where Alex and Matt were carefully removing precious stones from a pile of statues. "Fine," Alex replied, "This one had so many jewels on it, but I've finished stripping it now," he continued with satisfaction, throwing the now plain statue onto the growing pile beside him.

"It seems rather a waste," Gabriel said, looking sadly at the pile of statues on the ground, "I spent a long time carving out those gods. I know we've stopped making them now that we're followers of Jesus, but we could have sold these off first."

"Maybe," Matt said, "but I agree with your dad. We don't want anyone to carry on worshipping images of useless gods. They're best on the scrap heap."

"I suppose you're right," Gabriel said, "but they were popular in the market and brought in a lot of money.

Anyway, what I really came over to say was that you two can stop now." He picked up the basket of jewels, "There are plenty here for our workers to be getting on with for the next few days."

Thankfully, Alex and Matt put down their tools and wandered out of the workshop into the sunshine, leaving the sounds of tapping and scraping behind them. They sat down in the shade of an olive tree and for a short while said nothing.

Finally, Matt spoke, "I've been thinking," he began, "We need to make a plan."

Alex looked at his friend gratefully, "So you will help me, Matt?"

"Of course!" Matt replied, "I said so, didn't I? Now, this is the plan—We know that there were five ships that left the harbour and your sister was on one of them."

Alex sighed, "And there's no way of knowing which one. The one to Caesarea, Cyprus, Perga, Neapolis or Rome. My father and Gabriel questioned all the ship workers at the dock and none of them could say which ship they took."

"Right," Matt continued, "so that means we have to find ways to go on all of those ships and search in those five places."

"But the Romans may have travelled on by land, they could be anywhere by now," Alex protested.

"Ah, but you are forgetting three things," Matt said. "First, they are likely to want to show off your sister for some reason. Maybe they plan to sell her to a temple or to some rich Roman who wants a girl with special powers to bring good luck to his home. Secondly," Matt paused for a moment, looking a little embarrassed, "Secondly, Irana has got very beautiful red hair. She's a bit hard to hide, isn't she?"

"I see what you mean," Alex said, looking more cheerful, "Wherever we go we can ask people if they've seen her. But what's the third thing?"

Matt smiled, "You've forgotten that we can pray to a God who is great and who answers prayer!" he said quietly.

"I suppose so," Alex said, "but if God's so powerful, he could have stopped those people taking her in the first place. I wonder if he cares."

Chapter five

"**H**ey, Alex!"

Alex jumped. He had been concentrating on a particularly small detail in the panel he was painting and the sudden sound of the hissed whisper beside him gave him a fright.

"Matt!" he said, "don't do that! See I've spoiled the line I was painting." Annoyed, he quickly dabbed at the area he had painted so carefully. "Now I'll have to do it again."

"Sorry," Matt said, but not looking sorry at all. His usually pale face was flushed and his eyes were shining with excitement.

Alex finished dabbing at his painting and turned to his friend. "What is it?" he asked.

"My father has to go to Jerusalem to do business," Matt explained breathlessly, "And he wants me to go with him. We're taking the ship to Caesarea tomorrow! I've asked if you can come too."

"But even if your dad says yes, I doubt my father will let me go," Alex whispered doubtfully, glancing at Kostas who was working nearby. "He says we should leave Irana with God and just pray about her. He wouldn't agree to our plan, I'm sure."

"Don't worry," Matt reassured him. "My father will arrange everything. You'll see. Look!" He added, pointing across the workshop.

Alex looked and to his surprise saw Matt's father entering the workshop.

"Jonas!" Kostas exclaimed, "Peace be with you!"

"And peace be with you too," Jonas replied.

"Did you hear about the prophet who's come down from Jerusalem?" Kostas asked his friend.

"Yes," Jonas replied, "Agabus, I think his name is. God has told him we need to get ready for a famine over the whole Roman world. I suppose there'll be a shortage of food."

"They seem to think it'll be worse for the people in Judea so the Church is taking up a collection for the believers," Kostas said.

"Good idea," Jonas said, "I'll get some money to take to our next meeting."

"It's important to help each other," Kostas agreed "Oh, by the way," he continued, "Have you heard what people are calling us followers of Jesus?"

"I have," Jonas replied, "They're calling us Christians."

Kostas laughed, "I rather like it, even though I think they're trying to insult us."

Jonas smiled, "I agree. I wonder if the name will catch on." The two men chatted for a while and Alex watched, wondering how Jonas was going to arrange everything as Matt had promised.

At last Jonas said, "Actually, Kostas, I've come to ask a favour."

"What's that?" Kostas asked.

"Well, I have to go to Jerusalem. A merchant there is interested in buying some of my gem stones, quite a lot in fact and I need some extra help. Mattias is coming with me and I wondered if I could borrow Alex for a week or so."

Matt gripped his friend's arm as they waited for Kostas' reply.

"Well," Kostas said slowly, "I expect we could spare him. Actually, a change might do him good. Take his mind off his sister. It's upset him a lot you know. He's not even been practising his javelin throwing and you know how keen he was to get into the Antioch games. Of course, we're all upset ..." Kostas stopped, choking a little on the words before saying more firmly, "Yes, you're welcome to take him with you Jonas, I know you'll take care of him."

"Yes!" hissed Matt in triumph and Alex turned questioning eyes towards his friend. "How did you ...?" he asked.

Matt smiled, "Dad knows about our plan, I had to tell him Alex and he says he'll help as much as he can. But he says if you come, it will be to work for him. He doesn't want to deceive your father, so the less he knows about our search the happier he'll be."

Chapter six

S o it was that Alex began the search to find his sister. The sea trip from Antioch to Caesarea took four days which gave Alex and Matt plenty of time to ask all the crew if they had seen a girl with two Romans travelling to Caesarea. This was the headquarters of the Roman forces in that part of the world so it was possible that Irana had been taken there. But none of the sailors had seen her.

At the port they asked the ship workers if they had seen a 'red haired girl' arrive during the previous week, but no one had. They questioned everyone along the way enquiring at all the wayside inns from Caesarea to Jerusalem, but everyone they asked said the same.

"I'm almost certain they won't have brought Irana here," Alex said as he and Matt walked through the busy market in Jerusalem.

"Why are you so sure?" Matt asked, stepping sideways to avoid a stray dog searching for scraps that had fallen from the market stalls.

"Well!" Alex explained, "Look around you. This city is so different. Can you see any shrines or statues to any Greek or Roman gods like we have in Antioch? I've not even seen a statue of the Emperor. I can't imagine the people who live here being interested in my sister's special powers."

"I think you're right," Matt agreed, "but we still need to keep our eyes and ears open. Let's continue searching around the market. There are a several stalls at the far end where we've not looked."

For the hour or so the boys wandered in and out of the stalls where people were busy buying and selling. At intervals they would stop and ask the stall holders if they had seen Irana.

"There are hundreds of girls here in Jerusalem," one stall holder said, "what's so special about this one?"

"Come on Matt," Alex said at last, "let's look somewhere else, this is a waste of time."

"You're right," Matt replied, "no one seems to want to take us seriously. Let's go up towards the temple courts, there are always people wandering around up there."

Slowly, the two made their way towards the temple. As they went they asked some of the old men who sat in the doorways of their homes watching people going by. "They are more likely to see what goes on," Alex remarked. But none of them had seen Irana.

At the beautiful gate they stood gazing up at the magnificent building with its massive stone block pillars and golden roof shining brilliant white in the sunshine. Alex had never seen the temple before and was overwhelmed. "Wow!" was all he could say, "That is some building." And his friend agreed.

No one could remember seeing a girl looking like Irana, so after asking several more people at the gate of the temple the two friends agreed they should go back. They were very tired and hot so stopped at a well for a cooling drink before taking the road leading to the house where they had agreed to meet Jonas.

"Maybe the women at the meeting tonight can tell us if they've seen anything," Matt said.

"Good idea," Alex replied. "We're almost there, aren't we?" he asked, looking across at a house where a group of people were entering.

Matt nodded, "Yes, this is it. I expect my father is already here. He loves meeting with other believers in Jesus."

"There's Jonas," Alex said pointing to the doorway of a house ahead.

"So he is," Matt replied, "but he seems worried, I wonder what's wrong."

The two boys hurried over to where Matt's father stood. "What's happened?" Matt asked, looking at his father's pale face.

"It's James, John's brother. He is, or rather was, one of Jesus' first disciples." Jonas stopped and took a deep breath, "He's been killed."

"How? Why?" Alex asked, trying to imagine who would kill such a good, kind man.

"King Herod," Jonas said, "It seems he did it to please the people who hated Jesus—but that's not all," Jonas paused again and took another long breath, "He's put Peter in prison and is planning to kill him too."

Shocked, the two followed Jonas into the house. A maid only a little older than the boys locked the door behind them. "Thank you," Jonas said to the girl. "It's sad we have to lock ourselves in these days when we want to pray," he continued as they climbed the stairs. The large room upstairs was already full with a huge crowd of people sitting or standing. They had all heard the news and were gathered in groups around the upstairs room, praying for Peter.

Alex's head was spinning. How could God let his disciples be killed? he thought. If Jesus had beaten death and was alive now, why didn't he protect them? He remembered what his mother had said about God being great and good. Maybe he wasn't so great after all. What was the use of believing in a God who let his followers suffer? That didn't seem very good. And if God didn't stop King Herod killing James, what chance did Irana have?

Chapter seven

Jonas and Matt had already joined a prayer group near the doorway and Alex sat on the edge at the top of the stairs only half listening to the prayers. The whole room was filled with the sound of people praying. Every now and then one person's voice would rise above the others. It was many voices and yet one voice, pleading with God for Peter to be saved.

Because he was the nearest to the stairs, Alex heard the knocking at the door before anyone else. At first he thought it was a mistake, but then the knocking came again, louder this time. He supposed someone wanted to join the prayer meeting and stood up to open the door. But the girl who had let them in earlier had also heard and was already on her way to the stairs.

Idly, Alex watched as the girl went down the stone steps to the outside door. He couldn't really get too involved with all the prayers for Peter; he was too worried about Irana. Maybe God didn't care about her. Maybe he would let her die too.

Alex could hear a man's voice outside asking to be let in. The girl was at the door as he spoke but instead of opening the door Alex heard her cry out. Then she turned and came rushing back up the stairs almost tripping over the top step in her haste. "It's Peter!" she shouted and as the buzz of prayers died down she said again, her face shining with happiness, "Peter is at the door!"

For a moment there was silence and then one of the men said, "Come now Rhoda, you're out of your mind. I know we all want Peter to be here, but he's in prison chained to two soldiers with guards at the entrance of the prison."

"There is no way he can be at the door," someone else said, "You're imagining things."

Alex listened as the knocking continued and the girl called Rhoda continued to insist it was Peter.

"It must be his angel," one of the men finally said.

Why don't they open the door and find out? Alex thought impatiently, moving towards the stairs. By the time he was half way down, others who had finally decided to open the door were following behind him. He grasped the door handle and pulled it open. A big man stood there, smiling down at him. Alex had no idea who he was, but the men behind him saw immediately who it was and their shouts of joy left him in no doubt. It was Peter!

Everyone started talking at once wanting to know what had happened and how Peter had managed to escape. At last Peter waved them to be quiet and was able to explain.

It was an amazing story.

Peter had been sleeping as best he could while being chained to two soldiers, he explained, when suddenly he felt someone poke him. He woke up and saw an angel beside him and a light shining into the cell. "Quick, get up!" the angel said, and as he spoke the chains fell off Peter's wrists. Then the angel said, "Put on your clothes and sandals, wrap your cloak around yourself and follow me."

In a daze, Peter did what the angel said, although at the time he thought he must be dreaming. The soldiers beside him stayed asleep and he just walked out of the prison following the angel. They walked straight past the first guards then the second guards. When they got to the iron gates of the prison leading into the city they opened by themselves to let them out. Then after they'd walked the length of the street the angel disappeared.

"I know without a doubt that the Lord sent his angel and rescued me from Herod's clutches," Peter said.

After Peter had told his story he said, "Tell the brothers about this," and then he left the house. He didn't say where he was going which was probably just as well as they were sure Herod would be searching for him when his escape was discovered.

Alex stood staring out of the upstairs window, his back to the chattering people. He looked down at the dark street outside. Where was Irana? He was now sure she wasn't in Jerusalem. Would God let her be killed like James or would He send an angel to help her to escape? Alex had no doubt now that God could save her if He wanted to.

The question was, did God care?

Chapter eight

After the excitement of the Jerusalem visit, life in Antioch seemed quite boring. Alex was back in his usual routine at his father's workshop. He had been working for several hours painting an animal on a wall panel for one of their Roman customers.

"Can I go over to visit Matt?" Alex asked his father, "I think I've done as much as I can today."

Kostas bent down to look at Alex's work. The animal was a brown deer with long graceful legs and a gentle face. Alex was proud of his painting, although he knew that the finer details like the eyes and antlers would need to be painted by a steadier hand than his.

"That's coming on nicely," Kostas said smiling at his son.

"I need to get some javelin practice in," Alex continued earnestly, "Matt is going to see if I'm good enough to enter the javelin team for the games next month. I'm hoping to be chosen."

"Yes, you can go, Alex, you've worked hard today," Kostas said, "I'm glad you're practicing your javelin throwing again."

Alex picked up his brushes to wash and his father continued, "Once this panel is finished we will need to transport it to Cyprus."

"Cyprus?" Alex said quickly, "Is that where this panel is going?"

Kostas looked at his son in surprise, "Yes," he replied, "Why do you ask?"

Alex made an effort to keep his voice casual. "Oh, I like Cyprus," he said, "It's a nice island with cool rocks and a great beach. If you like, I can take the panel to our customer."

"Well," Kostas said, "I suppose you're old enough now to be trusted. As you've been involved in painting it you're more likely to look after it."

"Oh yes," Alex assured his father, "I'd take great care that it arrives in perfect condition."

"Good lad," Kostas said. "I'm glad to see you taking an interest in the business, at last. Once the panel is finished we'll see about you taking it to Cyprus. Maybe Matt would go with you."

"Ok," Alex said trying to keep the excitement out of his voice, "I'm off to see Matt now and I'll ask him."

"You can take an order with you to Jonas," Kostas said, "I need some more jewels so I'll give you a list for him."

Quickly, Alex set off towards the Jewish part of the city. Jonas had a large engraver's workshop and employed ten workers who carved and chiseled rough gemstones such as sardonyx, diamonds, rubies and sapphires. From the rough stones they produced jewelry and luxury items. Some of them were used to decorate sculptures and statues or decorative items like those made at Kostas' workshop. But some were shipped long distances to be sold to wealthy Romans around the empire.

"Hallo Alex," Jonas looked up as Alex entered the workshop. "What brings you here?"

"I've an order from my father," Alex replied, "and I've also come to see Matt."

Jonas took the list from Alex and after a quick glance at the items said, "Are you alright Alex? Not too disappointed that there was no news of your sister in Jerusalem?"

Alex looked up at Jonas. "I'm Ok, but … Jonas," he said, "Can I ask you something?"

Jonas smiled as he looked down at the boy, "Of course Alex, what is it?" he asked.

"Well," Alex said hesitantly, "Why do you think God saved Peter from being killed and not James? It seems so strange."

Jonas sighed, "Yes, it does seem strange." For a while Jonas was silent, narrowing his eyes in thought. "Do you know," he said at last, "I've heard that when Jesus was alive he also said some very strange things. One thing he said was that we will leap for joy when people hate and reject us, because of our great reward in heaven." Jonas paused, "I'm sure James is happier now than we can imagine," he said.

"And what about Irana?" Alex asked, "Do you think she might be killed too?"

Jonas sighed, "I wish I could say what you want to hear, Alex, but we just don't know do we?" There was another long pause and then Jonas said, "There was something else Jesus said to Peter once when he didn't understand what was going on. He said, 'You don't realise now what I'm doing, but later you will understand.' I think that may be true of Irana. So carry on praying and searching Alex. Don't give up. I'm sure God knows what he's doing."

Alex thanked Jonas and went in search of Matt who was sitting under the eucalyptus tree by the back door of his home.

"Am I glad to see you," Matt said laying down his chisel as he saw his friend. He frowned at the stone he had been carefully chipping away at. "Not very good," he sighed, "This is not as easy as you think."

"It must take a long time to learn to cut stones into jewels like your father does," Alex agreed, as he sat down thankfully beside his friend in the cool of the yard.

"Have a drink, boys," a voice called and they looked up to see Julia, Matt's mother holding out two mugs of water in the doorway. Gratefully, they took the mugs and Alex drank thirstily. "You do look hot Alex and you obviously want to tell Matt your news so I won't stop." Smiling, Julia took the empty mugs and went back inside.

"How did she know I had news?" Alex asked his friend.

Matt grinned, "She notices. You can't hide much from her! So—tell me?" he said, eagerly looking at Alex's flushed face.

"We're going to Cyprus Matt! And, maybe on this trip we'll get news of Irana!"

Chapter nine

"Have you got a spare shirt in your bag, Alex? Make sure you wear your hat in the sun or you'll get sunstroke. Here's your food for the journey. And take your goat hair coat for the evenings when it gets colder."

"Don't worry, mum. I've got everything I need." Alex laughed taking the large bag of food that she held out to him.

"All the same," Sophia said, "I am worried. It's the first time you've been on a trip alone and you could get into any kind of trouble. It's a good two days' sail to Cyprus and the sea can be dangerous if there's a storm. I'm surprised at your father allowing you to go."

"But Matt's coming with me and you've always said that he's more sensible than me," Alex replied.

"I know, I know," Sophia said, giving Alex a hug. "But I've already lost one child and I couldn't bear to lose you too. Off you go now," she said hastily pushing him away from her and blinking away a tear. "Your father is outside in the horse cart waiting to take you to the port and I can see Matt is already getting in. Take good care of that panel too."

Alex ran quickly to the cart and jumped up beside his friend and soon they were bumping along the road that would take them to Seleucia, the port of Antioch.

It was very early in the morning and the sun was only just coming up. The two boys sat in the cart watching as the horses carefully made their way along the stony ground. A dog lying on the track got up sleepily and staggered to the side as they passed. One or two market traders were on the road too, carrying fish and vegetables to their stalls before opening time. A little further on they passed the gymnasium and saw some athletes going in to do some running practice in the cool of the early morning. They were getting ready for the Antioch games.

"Hey, Alex!" one of them shouted and Kostas pulled the horses up so that they could hear what the man was saying. "I hear you've been chosen for the javelin competition next week. You'd better get lots of practice in!"

"I will!" Alex shouted back and bounced up from his seat laughing happily and waving at the man. He had been chosen for the games! Now all he needed to do was find Irana in Cyprus and bring her back to watch him compete. And if she was there he would certainly throw the javelin further than anyone else.

"Hang onto that panel," Kostas warned, "we're turning the corner!" Quickly, Alex settled back into his seat and tightened his hold on the wooden panel as the horses jerked the cart round the bend, away from Antioch and out onto the open road.

"Here we are," Kostas said at last as they came in sight of the port. "The wind seems good today. If the weather holds you could make the crossing to the island by tomorrow. Now don't forget," he continued firmly, "when you get there, ask for directions to the house of Sergius Paulus, the governor in charge of Cyprus. This panel is

33

for one of his workers, a man called Gregory. Once you've delivered the panel to him you can stay in an inn for a day and look around the capital, but please stay together. Then you are to come straight back."

"Ok, Father," Alex replied.

"Good lads," Kostas said, "Hop out now, we've arrived. Your ship is that one over there with the red sail. It's a Roman grain ship and the captain has agreed for you to travel with them. He's expecting you. Be good and keep that panel safe."

Carefully, Kostas handed the wooden panel, well wrapped in cloth, down to Matt who held one side while Alex took hold of the other. It was quite heavy for the boys, but together they were able to carry it, along with their bags, towards the waiting ship.

Once on board they found a good spot at the bow of the ship, made sure their precious parcel was secured safely and sat down on a large coil of rope ready to enjoy the crossing.

Alex looked out towards the blue sea with its streaks of purple and felt a quiver of excitement. Would they find his sister on the island of Cyprus? He looked back at the land where he could see his father, a lone figure, standing next to the horse cart watching them. Kostas waved goodbye and the boys watched his figure grow smaller and smaller until, with a final wave, he climbed up into the cart, turned the horses round and moved back towards Antioch.

Chapter ten

"We're almost there at last!" Alex exclaimed.

It had seemed a very long journey for Alex. He wasn't used to staying in one place and at times during the day he had wandered around the deck watching the sailors. They worked hard pulling the ropes of the sails to catch the wind. Sometimes, in the evening, the wind dropped and the boat moved slowly and Alex and Matt would watch shoals of little fish swimming past them.

At night they had laid down on the deck, covered in a thin blanket and had been rocked to sleep by the gentle rolling of the sea. They woke feeling very hungry and had enjoyed a breakfast of bread, dried olives and figs which Sophia had given them.

For some hours, they had been sailing alongside the beautiful island of Cyprus. The wind had been blowing in the right direction for the whole journey and they were making good time. From the side of the ship they could see the long sandy beaches and coves surrounded by rocks. Now and then there were sand dunes, some quite large, covered with green shrubs.

"It looks so peaceful," Matt said as they watched the sailors smoothly guiding the ship in and out of the rocks which seemed to suddenly appear as they got closer to the shore.

"Yes," Alex agreed, "but I bet it's more exciting when the sea is rough! Imagine sailing between these rocks when the wind is blowing the ship all over the place!"

"Maybe," Matt replied doubtfully, "but I think I prefer it like this!"

It was early morning now and the only living creatures they could see were the occasional wild donkey or the sea birds sitting on the shore. The sun was beginning to rise and the sky was turning a gentle pink. The view was amazing with different coloured rocks emerging from the clear, blue water.

"What a shame we have to search for Irana," Matt remarked, "I'd love to spend a day climbing those rocks and swimming in the bay."

"Me too," Alex sighed, "but maybe if we find her we can do it on the way back."

The boys were quiet for a while. They silently knew that even if they found Irana the next difficulty would be in persuading her to come back with them. But neither of them voiced their fears.

"There's the port of Paphos," Alex said at last, pointing ahead where they could see a crowd of boats with different coloured sails anchored up for the night. "And look Matt, over there is Aphrodite's Rock!"

Matt followed Alex's pointed finger and saw a large rock, rising from the sea near to the shore. "Just looks like another rock to me," he said, "What's so special about that one?"

"Don't you know anything Matt?" Alex said in disgust, "That's the birth place of Aphrodite, the Greek goddess of love and beauty. It's where she rose from the waves.

There's a temple here where people worship her, although, they probably call her Venus as that's her Roman name."

Matt looked at his friend in amazement. "Do you believe in her then?" he asked.

"Not now," Alex said, "But of course I used to, before I heard about Jesus. I believed in all the different gods. Everyone did."

"Incredible," Matt said, shaking his head. "Us Jews have always known there was only one God; the one who made the world."

The boy's discussion came to an abrupt halt as the ship suddenly stopped and several sailors jumped ashore with ropes to tie the ship to the mooring posts on the harbour wall.

"Ok, lads." The boys turned as they heard the captain speaking to them. "I suggest you get off the boat first so that you don't get in the way," he said to them. His voice was harsh, but he was smiling as he spoke. "It will take us a while to get the cargo off and we don't want to be tripping over you."

Quickly, the boys gathered up the panel and their overnight bags and calling thank you to the sailors, made their way down the gang plank and onto dry ground. They stood for a while uncertain what to do next, watching as the sailors began to unload the bags of grain to the waiting merchant below.

"We're in the way here, Alex," Matt said, "Let's go up onto the track ahead, I can see a well where we can fill our water skins, I'm dying for a drink. And then we can ask the way to the governor's house.

Chapter eleven

As the two approached the well, they saw a group of women filling up their pots of water ready to carry back to their homes. They put the panel down carefully on the ground and stood back politely waiting for the women to finish.

The women seemed in no hurry though. "Have you heard the news?" one of them said to the others.

"Do you mean about the new god?" they answered.

"Yes, only this Jesus god is something altogether different, they say," the first woman replied.

Matt and Alex looked at each other and smiled knowingly. So the news about Jesus had spread over to Cyprus too.

"It's these teachers who have come over from Antioch," the woman continued. "They've travelled right across Cyprus telling people about this Jesus."

"They're making amazing claims," another woman said, "They say this Jesus is the god of the whole world, but it sounds pretty far fetched to me. We all know that the mountains, the woods, the rivers and the seas all have their own god. How can there be one god over everything?"

"Impossible!" a new woman joined in, heaving up the bucket from the well as she spoke, "my grandfather says his uncle saw Poseidon, the god of the sea, near to our coast. He was in his chariot being pulled by white horses."

"Hmmm, I don't know about that," said the first, looking doubtful, "But I want to hear more about this Jesus."

"What are their names? These teachers?" asked a woman who had just finished filling her pot.

"One is called Barnabas. He seems to be the leader. And there's a man called Saul and another called Mark. The whole town is talking about them. It seems Sergius Paulus is interested in hearing more from them too."

"Sergius Paulus," Matt whispered, "Isn't his the house we need to find?"

Alex nodded, "I'll go and ask them where he lives," he whispered back.

The women were slowly moving away from the well, so while Matt turned the handle to pull up the bucket from the well to fill their water skins, Alex went to question the women.

"The house is up there," Alex said as he came back to his friend. He pointed behind them towards a hill, "You can actually see it from here, it's that huge villa at the top."

"Yes, I can see," Matt replied, in between taking gulps of water, "It looks a bit of a climb. I shall be glad to get rid of this panel, it is heavy!"

Carefully, carrying the wooden panel between them, the two began the climb up the hill towards the grand villa. After a while, the rough stone path changed to a smooth walkway leading to paved steps with flowering shrubs and palm trees on either side.

As they reached the main entrance they stopped to catch their breath. They looked back the way they had come. From here they could see the white and red sails of the boats in the harbour below and the Mediterranean Sea spread out like a blue carpet in the distance.

"What a view!" Matt exclaimed.

They turned to take in the fine building in front of them with its huge courtyard. There was a magnificent fountain in the centre, its spray falling on a statue of Aphrodite. A group of black geese were strolling between the palm trees. Around the courtyard were various other buildings where slaves who worked in the house lived.

"Wow!" Alex exclaimed, "This is a bit grand!"

Matt nodded, "It's more a palace than a villa," he agreed, "How will we find Gregory here?"

Alex considered, "I think we should go to the back entrance and ask," he said, so they picked up the panel and cautiously stepped into the courtyard, making their way to what looked like the servant's entrance to the villa.

Chapter twelve

As it turned out, it wasn't difficult to find Gregory. He was doing an inspection of the kitchen area when the two enquired. They were impressed to see the tall man, dressed in a long blue cotton shirt with a leather belt around his waist, who came to greet them. He led them into a separate room where they handed over the precious piece of work.

"I hope you haven't damaged it on the journey," Gregory said as he opened the parcel.

"We've been very careful," Alex assured him and watched proudly as Gregory stood back to inspect the painted panel with the graceful deer surrounded by flowers and trees.

"It's good," Gregory said, "I'm pleased with that—it will look very fine in my living area. Thank your father for me." He turned as someone in the house called his name. "I'm needed inside. Please get a drink from the kitchen before you go and see yourselves out." With a swift movement he was gone, leaving Matt and Alex alone.

The boys stood for a moment staring round at the room they were in. It was a kind of reception room which led into a corridor. There was no one around so without discussing it, they quietly stepped into the corridor leading towards the main part of the house. All over the walls and ceilings were beautiful carvings and paintings. Even the floors had beautiful pictures of strange gods surrounded by vine trees and peacocks and animals all made from small mosaic tiles. It was like being in another world.

They were so busy looking at the floor that they hadn't realised the corridor had opened out into a large room where many people were gathering. The sudden noise of the people made them look up in alarm. Everyone was turned towards another doorway as if waiting for someone to come in. No one took any notice of the two boys.

At that moment, they saw three men over the other side of the room that they recognized immediately. Matt put his mouth near to Alex's ear. "Look!" he hissed, "That's Barnabas, Mark and Saul!"

"So it is!" Alex said, "And who's this coming in? He must be the governor. Look at his clothes!" Matt looked. The man was dressed in a white toga with a purple border which had been wound around his body. On his feet were beautifully made leather sandals.

He walked slowly into the room, his eyes fixed all the time on Barnabas and Saul.

Behind Sergius Paulus came other men who were obviously his attendants, there to serve him. One of them came to stand at the governor's side. He was a strange looking man and was watching Barnabas and Saul suspiciously. When Alex saw him he felt a shiver of fear. His eyes reminded Alex of Irana's eyes on that fateful day outside Agatha's house.

There was silence in the room, then the governor spoke, "Thank you for coming Barnabas and Paul. I've sent for you because I want to hear the word of God that you are teaching around these parts."

Alex looked questioningly at Matt, "Paul?" he whispered, "Why Paul all of a sudden?"

"Because," Matt whispered back, "that's his Roman name—he's a Roman citizen, remember? It sounds better here than Saul."

They listened as first Barnabas and then Paul began to explain to the governor how Jesus had come into the world to die for the sins of the people and to free them from the fear of false gods. Every now and then the man beside Sergius Paulus frowned and shook his head.

Then the boys noticed the governor turning to talk to the man whose name was Elymas. Their voices were too low to hear, but it was obvious from his face that Elymas was trying to convince Sergius Paulus that Paul was talking nonsense. The governor was looking from Elymas to Paul as if unsure who to believe.

For a while there was a lot of arguing going on. Various people joined in the argument and the governor was beginning to look irritated. Then suddenly, Paul seemed to stand taller. His face seemed filled with a determination which had not been there before. He looked straight at Elymas and said, "You're a child of the devil and an enemy of everything that is right!"

A gasp went round the room as Paul continued, "You are full of deceit and tricks. Now the hand of the Lord is against you. You are going to be blind and for a time you won't be able to see the light of the sun!"

Everyone watched in horror as Elymas' eyes seemed to cloud over. With a curse he rubbed at his eyes and it was obvious to everyone that he couldn't see. Blindly, he reached out his hands, groping around for someone to help him. At last one of the servants took pity on him, took his hand and led him out of the room, almost touching Alex and Matt as they passed.

The governor spoke at last. "Your teaching is amazing! I can see it's the truth. I believe in your Lord Jesus!"

What happened next the boys didn't know because one of the servants suddenly noticed them. He led them firmly out of the house the same way Elymas had gone just a few minutes before.

Chapter thirteen

Alex and Matt were silent as they left the governor's house. It was beginning to get dark, so they walked back to the centre of Paphos and found a bed at the Aphrodite Inn. They lay awake for a long time after they had settled for the night. Matt was so excited about what they'd seen but Alex was lost in his own thoughts.

"Wasn't it amazing Alex?" Matt whispered from his bed. "To think, that the governor of Paphos has become a Christian! When he saw the magician go blind he had to admit the power of Jesus." When Alex didn't reply Matt continued, "Is there something wrong Alex?"

After a silence Alex asked quietly as if talking to himself, "Would Paul say Irana was a child of the devil? Will she be punished too?"

Matt gasped. "Of course not!" he said, but there was uncertainty in his voice. After thinking for a few moments Matt went on, "Elymas tried to turn the governor against Jesus. Irana never did that!"

"But she wasn't very interested in Jesus when the rest of us became Christians," Alex continued.

"No, Alex!" Matt said again, "Irana was led astray by that evil Agatha. If we find her, everything will be fine."

"We must find her," Alex said urgently.

After a while Matt fell asleep but poor Alex's thoughts kept going round and round in his head until the sun began to rise and he at last fell into an uneasy sleep.

Next day Matt and Alex spent the morning wandering round Paphos asking everyone they met if they had seen a girl with beautiful red hair in the company of two Romans. They hung around outside the governor's villa watching people going in and out and checking the women working in the compound. But none of them was Irana.

Finally, in the afternoon they wandered sadly, down to the harbour to pick up the boat to take them back to Antioch. Matt was about to step onto the ship when Alex grabbed his arm, "Look Matt!" he almost shouted in his excitement, "Over there, getting onto that other ship!" Matt looked in the direction of his friend's finger and saw a girl with bright red hair disappearing into the ship. "Did you see her?" Alex asked, "It's Irana! I'm sure of it!" The next minute Alex was running towards the ship and before Matt could catch up with him he was climbing onto the deck. At that moment there was a shout from the Captain, "Cast off!" and the sails began to catch the wind.

"Wait for me!" Matt panted and Alex reached down and pulled his friend onto the ship as it began to pull away from the shore.

"Phew! Only just in time," Alex said, "Come on, Matt," he continued impatiently, "Let's go and find Irana."

Eagerly the two boys crossed the deck and began looking for the red haired girl. This was a bigger ship than the one to Antioch. It was carrying grain as well as a large number of passengers.

"Alex!" Matt suddenly said to his friend after they had been searching for a while among the passengers on deck, "You do realise that we haven't got permission to be on this ship and we don't even know where it's going!"

"You're right, Matt," Alex said looking worried, "We'd better hide. If the captain sees us we could be in trouble."

"Let's go down into the hold," Matt suggested, "We can hide amongst the sacks of grain."

Quickly, the boys went down the wooden steps into the bottom of the ship. They stood blinking for a while until their eyes got used to the dark and then looked around for a good place. "Over here," Matt said pointing to a place where several sacks of grain were stowed. "If we move two of these over a bit we can get onto the floor of the ship and be completely hidden from sight."

"Now what?" Alex asked after they had settled themselves down into their hiding place. "How are we going to find Irana while we're hiding?"

"I'm not sure," Matt replied, "but I do know I don't want to be found by the captain. I once heard about a stowaway who was thrown overboard when he was caught."

Alex trembled, "We should stay where we are for the time being," he said. "When we get to wherever we're going we should be able to see Irana as she gets off."

Chapter fourteen

It seemed as if they had been hiding amongst the sacks of grain for hours. Fortunately, they had brought some food with them for the journey, but they had eaten it a long time ago. They had also dozed for a while as there was nothing else to do.

A sudden jolt woke them. A sack of grain had fallen against their legs and the boys could feel the ship swaying from side to side.

"I think we're in for a storm," Matt whispered.

Alex agreed. "I'm glad this is a big ship," he whispered back, "it's a lot more stable than a smaller one."

For a while the two boys sat crouched between the sacks of grain listening to the wind and the splashing of the waves against the side of the ship. Anxiously, they looked at each other as the wind grew stronger and the ship began to be tossed around.

Above them on the deck they could hear the captain shouting instructions to the sailors as they tried to hold the sails steady. The sacks of grain began to slide around and every now and then they were squashed between them. Then, to their dismay the boys realised that the ship was beginning to leak. Just a small amount of water at first, but slowly increasing and slopping to and fro as the ship swayed from side to side.

On deck they heard the Captain giving orders. "Pull down the sails!" he shouted, "and throw out the sea anchor!" The boys held their breath as the sailors ran around above them obeying his instructions.

"What shall we do?" said Alex, looking down at the water splashing at their feet. "It's not safe down here."

Before Matt could answer they heard the Captain calling, "We need to make the ship lighter! Throw the cargo overboard!" With dismay the boys watched as four sailors jumped down into the hold and began to haul sacks of grain up onto the deck for the sailors above to throw overboard. They were going to be discovered.

One of the sailors grabbed a sack next to Matt and Alex and saw the two miserable boys standing together. "Hey!" the sailor yelled to his partner, "Stowaways!" The other sailor turned to look at them, "It's just a couple of kids," he replied and carried on with his task.

The first sailor spoke to the boys, "You'd better make yourselves useful unless you want to be killed."

Matt and Alex looked around feverishly wondering what they could do to help. At that moment two buckets were thrown down the hold and someone shouted, "Start bailing!" Quickly, Alex grabbed a bucket and filled it with the water lapping around his ankles. "Get up the steps, Matt," he said, "and I'll pass it up to you to throw overboard."

Matt scuttled up the wooden steps and emerged on the deck wondering what would happen when the Captain saw him. But the Captain was far too busy trying to keep the ship facing the wind so that it wouldn't roll over, to notice the frightened boy.

For what seemed an age, Alex passed bucket after bucket of water up to Matt who emptied it overboard before dropping the empty bucket down to Alex again. The weeks of javelin practice meant that Alex was able to easily swing the heavy buckets up to Matt. His friend was smaller and not as strong, but he didn't stop despite the pain in his arms.

The howling wind and rain were pounding the ship and both of them were soaked to the skin but neither took any notice. They carried on with their task as the sailors ran around them lightening the ship as they threw the precious cargo overboard.

"Well done, lads," one of the sailors said as he pushed past with the final sack of grain. "You're doing a fine job there."

Everyone was very relieved when they heard the Captain say at last, "Land! I see land! Hold on everyone, I think we're going to make it." The next few minutes were very confusing as sailors worked to turn the ship into the bay. The passengers held their breath as with a final lurch they reached the harbour.

"Passengers off first," the Captain ordered and the passengers came quickly from their cabins and hurried to jump ashore from the ship that was still rocking and swaying in the wind. Alex and Matt watched eagerly in the shadows to see the girl they were sure was Irana. They were slightly surprised to see Barnabas, Saul and Mark get off the ship. They hadn't realised they were on board too.

"There she is," Matt exclaimed and they watched as the red haired girl came towards them. Then as she got closer he said quietly, "Oh no!"

"It's not her," Alex cried in disappointment, "Oh Matt, it's not Irana! I was so sure I'd found her."

Chapter fifteen

Alex's loud cry made the Captain turn round and they saw his brown wrinkled face glaring down at them. "Where did you two come from?" he said harshly, "I don't remember you paying to come aboard."

Matt thought quickly, "We're sorry sir but we got onto the wrong boat at Paphos. We wanted to go to Seleucia."

The Captain looked at the boys more closely and then asked in a more gentle voice. "Are you the two who've been bailing out the ship?" Alex and Matt looked up at him with pleading eyes and nodded.

"You did well," the Captain said in his gruff voice smiling down at Matt who was rubbing his painful arms. "Your hard work helped to keep us afloat."

Matt gulped. The Captain looked a bit friendlier now, so he asked, "Could you please tell us where we are?"

The Captain grunted, "You're a long way from Seleucia, you're in Perga in Pamphylia."

Alex finally found his voice, "Please sir, can you tell us how to get to Antioch from here."

"Well now," the Captain said, "You won't be going anywhere in this weather. I suggest you both follow the other passengers to the 'Perga Inn' and get some rest. Do you have enough money to stay there?"

The boys nodded and the Captain went on, "Hopefully, this storm will have blown itself out by tomorrow morning and you can take the boat of a friend of mine that's sailing to the port at Antioch. Come down to the docks mid-morning tomorrow and I'll see what I can arrange for you. It's the least I can do for two stowaways who helped to get my ship safely into the harbour." With a smile that twisted up his wrinkled face even more, he went back into the ship to assess the damage.

The two miserable boys did as the Captain had said and followed the other wet and bedraggled passengers into the welcoming inn just a few minutes' walk away. "Come by the fire, lads," the kindly innkeeper's wife said, "You're soaked to the skin." Thankfully, they sat around the fire and drank a cup of warm wine and slowly felt the life coming back into their chilled bodies.

Everyone around them was talking about the voyage and how they had thought they would perish in the storm. Inside the inn were statues of the various gods and some of the passengers were bowing to the little statues and presenting flowers and fruit as a thank you to them. Across the crowd Alex could see Barnabas and Saul bowing their heads and he guessed they were thanking God.

"We're lucky to be alive," Alex said and his friend agreed. "We could easily have drowned," Matt said, "Or been thrown overboard as stowaways."

"It's all my fault we're in this mess," Alex said sadly, "We haven't found Irana and here we are miles from home. Our parents will be so worried about us."

Matt put his arm round his friend for a moment. "Never mind Alex, God has taken care of us so far, so I'm sure he'll get us home safely."

"Do you think we can trust that Captain to remember to help us tomorrow?" Alex said doubtfully.

"I'm sure he will," Matt assured him, "And we've found out that Irana didn't go to Cyprus, which is progress."

Alex gave his friend a weak smile, "You're right, Matt, we mustn't give up," but his voice didn't sound very convincing.

The murmur of voices around them had quietened down as people began to get warm and sleepy. Some were dozing off and others were sitting silently, staring into the fire.

The only ones still talking were Paul, Barnabas and Mark.

Every now and then Matt and Alex could hear a few words of their whispered conversation. Mark's sounded upset and it seemed as if Barnabas was trying to calm him down. He was looking sad but Paul seemed quite annoyed.

Matt nudged Alex. "Did you hear that Alex?"

"Not really," Alex replied, "Something about going back to Jerusalem. You've got better ears than me, Matt. What are they saying?"

"It looks as if Mark wants to go home," Matt answered. "He doesn't want to travel with them any longer."

"Well!" Alex said wearily, "I don't blame him either. After all, we heard that Jesus could stop the wind and waves with just a word. I wonder why, if God is so great, he lets his followers get into so much trouble."

"My father says we live in a broken world and we can't expect to have an easy life," Matt answered his friend.

"He told me that Jesus once warned his disciples to expect suffering if they wanted to follow him."

At last the two boys were dry and warm and were beginning to feel drowsy so they laid their exhausted bodies down on their mats and were soon fast asleep.

Chapter sixteen

It was very early when Alex was shaken awake by Matt.

"It's too early to get up," grumbled Alex, "the Captain said mid-morning we should meet him."

"Yes, I know that," Matt said impatiently, "but do you know where we are?"

"We're a long way from home and our parents will be mad with us," Alex replied.

"We're in Perga!" Matt continued, "Perga! That's where one of the ships was heading. Remember? It's one of the places we said we needed to go to look for Irana."

"So it is," Alex said, suddenly wide awake, "and we have until lunch time to search for her."

The two friends ate a quick breakfast and went out immediately. First they asked at all the Inns in Perga, but apart from the girl who had been on their ship, no one could remember any other girl with bright red hair.

"Go to the temple of the great goddess Artemis," someone advised, pointing towards an impressive white building a short distance away. "There are several fortune tellers there. That's where you'll find her if she's in Perga."

Eagerly the two boys ran towards the temple. They stopped for a moment and admired the beautiful building with its tall columns carved with a statue of the goddess, a golden bow and arrow in her hand and a hunting dog at her feet. Then, as they approached the entrance, sure enough there all around the temple steps were women and girls covered in dark shawls. They were telling people's fortunes in exchange for a gold coin. Some were reading a person's palms, others appeared to be in a trance and were muttering strange sounds.

The boys shivered. Quickly, they ran from one to the other, looking under their shawls to see their faces and hair. But to their disappointment none of them were Irana.

They then went to the dockside and asked the harbour master and the old fishermen who sat around watching the ships coming in and out. They all shook their heads, "We notice any pretty girl who arrives," one of the old men said with a leer, "but unfortunately most of the people are men." His friends cackled and Alex and Matt walked away in disgust.

"I hope the Captain hasn't forgotten us," Matt said when mid-morning came and they stood looking at the broken ship on which they had arrived the previous evening.

"I hope not too," Alex agreed, "We don't have enough money to pay the fare back."

They needn't have worried, for the Captain was as good as his word. As soon as he saw the boys he took them to his friend who was due to set sail for Antioch.

"Here are the two stowaways I told you about," the Captain said, as he handed them over. "I don't think they'll give you any trouble."

The other laughed as they climbed on board. "I think they'll just be glad to be going home," he agreed.

It was a very different day. The sun was shining, the wind was blowing gently and the sea was calm. All that could be seen to remind them of the storm were the broken masts and torn sails on various boats around the harbour.

The Antioch ship needed a few repairs, but in no time at all they were sailing out of Perga and moving swiftly with the wind behind them. The sea looked beautiful today and seemed to be covered in thousands of jewels as the sun sparkled on its blue surface.

Alex and Matt were lost in their own thoughts and talked very little on the voyage. It was true, both of them were just longing to be home.

Chapter seventeen

They arrived back in Antioch as the afternoon sun was going down. No one was there to meet them and Alex remembered that his father had probably met the ship from Cyprus the previous night. How worried he must have been when he saw they weren't on it.

Hastily, the two boys hitched a lift with a cart that was going into town and as soon as they arrived in Antioch they said goodbye to each other and quickly ran to their homes.

As Alex ran up the path into the kitchen his mother let out a scream of joy and pain and threw her apron over her head. "Oh you bad boy!" she cried, "Where have you been? I've been so worried." She emerged from her apron and pulled Alex into her arms not waiting for him to answer. "I thought you were dead! I thought I'd lost another precious child."

Alex held onto his mother and said nothing for a while. Then she pushed him away and ran to the door of the workshop. "Kostas! Gabriel! He's back! Thank God, he's home."

The two men came quickly into the kitchen and having reassured themselves that Alex really was there, they sat down wearily looking at him. The relief on their faces made Alex feel even guiltier than before.

"What happened?" Kostas said at last, "Tell us everything."

Alex gulped, "Well!" he began, "We delivered the panel safe and sound and Gregory was very happy with it."

He paused, hoping Kostas would be pleased, but his father just said, "And?"

"And Matt and I had a day in Paphos, like you said we could," Alex went on, "and then we went to the harbour to catch the ship back home."

"So why weren't you on it?" Gabriel asked. "It was a rough night, but the ship arrived Ok. We thought you must have gone overboard in the storm."

"We didn't take that ship," Alex began.

"Why ever not?" Sophia said, "Your father told you to come straight back. It's not like you to be so disobedient. I knew I shouldn't have let you go alone."

The anger in her voice found an echo inside Alex and he suddenly lifted his head and looked at his family. His face was very red and his eyes were flashing.

"You don't understand!" he shouted. "I can't just sit and pray. I have to find her! And I won't rest until I do!" Then he flung himself down on the mat on the floor and burst into tears.

Sophia, Kostas and Gabriel looked at each other, puzzled. "What is he talking about?" Gabriel asked.

"Don't you see?" Sophia exclaimed. "He's been looking for Irana."

"So that's why he's been so eager to travel," Kostas said, "It all makes sense now."

As they looked at the sobbing boy they all had tears in their eyes. "Poor little boy," Gabriel said at last, "And poor little Irana. Whatever has happened to her? Will we ever know?"

Bit by bit the family got the story from Alex. How he and Matt had agreed that they would look for Irana together and how they had planned to go to all the places that the ship may have carried her.

After Alex had told the whole story, he was given a good meal and a bath and tucked up into his warm bed where he fell asleep as soon as his tired head touched the pillow.

His family stayed up quite late that night talking and praying and wondering what could be done for Irana.

Chapter eighteen

For the next few days Alex didn't have time to mope. He got up very early each morning and spent an hour practising his javelin throw. After his morning in the work shop he spent another hour practising. Sometimes, Matt came to help him and it was always easier to practise when Alex had his friend to urge him on. Also Matt would pick up the javelin after he had thrown it and return it to him which meant he could get more throws into less time.

At last, the day of the Antioch games arrived. Kostas had decided to close his workshop for the day so that he and Gabriel could go along to watch the games.

"I wish I could come to see you," Sophia complained, "but they don't allow married women into the stadium."

Kostas laughed, "I wouldn't want you to see all those naked men!"

"Nonsense," Sophia said crossly, "I don't want to see the men's races. It's the boys' events I'm interested in. I only wanted to see Alex perform. Well off you go lads and tell me all about it later."

Calling goodbye to Sophia, Alex and Matt walked quickly down the hill towards the gymnasium. Kostas and Gabriel followed at a slower pace behind. "Go on without us," they called. "We'll be watching you from the front of the stadium."

They entered the grand entrance to the gymnasium along with many other boys. "Most of the competitors are older than you are, Alex," Matt said to his friend.

"I know," Alex said, "But I'm still going to beat them if I can!"

The atmosphere in the stadium was amazing. This was the first games that Matt had ever seen and he was fascinated by all the different events. The main events were on the running track, but there was also wrestling and boxing, chariot racing, horse racing and long jump. In between the sports events there was a dance event and someone doing some clever acting and miming.

At last it was time for the javelin and discus throwing events and Alex joined the other competitors in a line waiting for his turn.

Matt watched from a short distance away as the first boy ran towards the line and threw his javelin. Twenty seven point four meters. Alex glanced back at Matt who gave him the thumbs up. Alex could certainly throw further than this. The second and third boys made their throw twenty nine point thirty six meters and thirty one point twenty meters. Better, but still short of Alex's record. Then a very tall athletic looking boy took his turn. He ran up to the line, accelerating as he went, his javelin held in a steady horizontal line. The crowd held their breath as the javelin left his hand and sailed into the air. It was a beautiful throw thirty four point five meters. The crowd roared and clapped. Matt shook his head. Alex wouldn't be able to beat that.

Then it was Alex's turn. He looked very serious, pausing for a moment as he prepared his run up, then he began to run. His javelin was straight and absolutely still as he ran, his eyes looking steadily over his left shoulder. A perfect position, thought Matt. Everyone watched as Alex threw the javelin with all his might. It was a very good throw but as it landed Matt could see it was slightly less than the previous boy had achieved. Thirty point forty eight meters. All the same, Alex looked very pleased. He had beaten his own record and he had come second in the competition.

"I'm proud of you, son," Kostas said as they left the stadium. "Second prize at your first Antioch games." "Very well done, Alex," Gabriel said and Matt slapped his friend on the back. Alex grinned happily. "Next year I'll be the winner," he promised.

Later after celebrating with his family, Alex walked with Matt to his home across the city. They had both fallen silent and were thinking their own thoughts.

Alex sighed. "I wish Irana had been at the games to see me," he said at last.

"Yes!" Matt agreed, "Some how you miss people more when something good happens."

"My mother has forbidden any more travelling," Alex said sadly.

"Mine too," Matt said gloomily.

"We'll have to find a way," Alex went on as they parted company, "I can't give up now."

Chapter nineteen

*I*t was a week or two later and the two friends were sitting in their favourite spot under the eucalyptus tree near to Matt's home.

"We must think of a plan," Matt said. "Our mothers won't let us go anywhere out of Antioch alone, but they might let us go with someone else. First we need to decide where our next destination is and then we must look for our chance."

Alex scratched his head, "We know Irana is not in Jerusalem, Cyprus or Perga. It is possible she could have arrived in Perga without those fishermen seeing her and gone on to one of the Roman cities like Lystra. Apart from that the other two places are Neapolis or Rome." He sighed, "Are we wasting our time, Matt? Is it impossible?"

"My father says, 'nothing is impossible with God,'" Matt said, then paused as he thought of Irana. How beautiful and gentle she had been before she got involved with Agatha. It was dreadful to think what might be happening to her now. He took a deep breath then said again in a determined voice, "Nothing is impossible with God, so I say we carry on."

Their conversation was interrupted by the sound of a horse plodding up towards the house. They watched as the man came closer. "Oh! It's the post," Alex said, "Looks as if your father has a letter."

"Now that's a good way to travel," Matt said thoughtfully, "those horses travel miles delivering mail around the empire. Did you know that they can carry a letter fifty miles in a day?"

"How does that help?" Alex replied gloomily, "We're too young to get a job as postmen."

Jonas came out at that moment and eagerly took the letter from the horseman. He could read both Greek and Hebrew and often received letters from Peter or Barnabas to be read out to the believers in Antioch.

"This is from Barnabas," he said to the boys, "I expect it's news of the work in Asia." He sat down beside the boys and unrolled the parchment and was silent for a while as he read. The boys watched his face but it was difficult to see if the news was good or bad, so many different expressions passed over his face.

"Well!" Matt asked at last impatiently, "How are they and what's going on?"

Jonas looked up. "It is good news and bad news" he said. "Mark decided not to continue with them and has returned to Jerusalem which is sad."

"Yes, we know that," Alex said, "Is that the bad news? What's the good news?"

"The good news is that many people in Pisidian Antioch and Iconium now believe in Jesus. The Jews welcomed them and invited them to speak in the synagogue. So Paul explained to them from the scriptures how Jesus was the one who had been promised long ago. Lots of people—both

Jews and Gentiles—have become Christians. But then ..."
Jonas paused sighing.

"But then ...?" Matt prompted him.

"But then some of the Jews got jealous and stirred
up trouble. Paul and Barnabas said to them that if they
wouldn't accept the truth then they would preach to the
Gentiles instead. It seems they got thrown out of Pisidian
Antioch and nearly got stoned to death in Iconium."

"Phew!" Alex said, "So they're coming home, I suppose,
to recover."

"Not them!" Jonas said smiling, "They sound in very
good spirits. They say they're going on to Lystra to tell the
people there the good news about Jesus. Hmmm ..." Jonas
was silent for a while, thinking, then, he looked hard at
the two boys. "I've some business to do in Lystra. This
might be a good time to go. I'd like to be able to encourage
the brothers and could take some provisions to them at the
same time."

Alex and Matt stared at Jonas and both opened their
mouths as if to speak but Jonas held up his hand. "Don't
say anything!" he commanded, "let's just wait and see."

Chapter twenty

"Alex, can I have a word with you?" Alex looked up from his work on a new panel for a customer, as Kostas came and sat beside him. His father looked at the two skinny dogs sniffing each other's noses on the panel and smiled approvingly. Alex looked up enquiringly. "I've been talking to Jonas," his father began and then stopped and asked, "Alex, are you and Matt still talking about searching for Irana?"

"Of course!" Alex said, flushing, "We will never stop looking for her. She is my sister, and Matt's friend. How can we give up?"

Kostas looked down at the determination on his son's face. "Jonas seems to think we should let you try. I'm not at all sure about it and your mother is very unhappy …" He trailed off while Alex held his breath. "Jonas is going to Lystra on a business trip. He's taking the horse and cart and is willing to take you and Matt with him."

Alex jumped to his feet and clasped his hands together. "Oh father, please, please let me go!" he cried.

"It would only be for a few days," Kostas said. "And you would have to promise not to wander anywhere on your own without Jonas knowing. Your mother was out of her mind with worry when you missed your ship from Cyprus."

"I promise, I promise!" Alex cried. "Oh thank you, thank you father."

"Alex," Kostas continued, "I know you think that we should be searching and trying to find Irana as you are, but your mother and I pray every day that Irana will be kept safe. We believe that God is great and good and is looking after her. Do you believe that too?"

Alex sighed. "I know God is great. I saw how he got Peter out of prison and how he made that evil magician go blind. And I believe he is good but ..." his voice trailed off.

"But?" asked his father, putting his hand on his son's shoulder. "But what?"

Alex sighed again, "Well, I know Jesus came to take away our sins so that we can go to heaven when we die," he said, "but what about our life on earth while we're alive? Does he care that we've lost Irana? Maybe he's too great to bother about an ordinary family like ours."

Kostas thought for a moment a frown creasing his forehead. "I think he does care," he said at last. "Remember some of the things we've heard about Jesus. When he lived on earth he cared about all the people who were old and poor and ill. He even cared about really bad people. Why should he be any different now he's in heaven?"

"So then, why did Jesus let James be killed or Irana be kidnapped?" Alex asked, "I'm not so sure that He does always care."

Kostas nodded. "I know how you feel. We don't understand why things happen but I'm sure God will bring something good out of our trouble if we let him."

"Maybe," Alex said, but there was doubt in his voice.

"Now hurry and finish painting those dogs." Kostas said briskly, "When you've done that you need to go to see Matt and make plans for your trip to Lystra. Jonas wants to leave in the morning."

At this Alex brightened up. With shining eyes Alex looked gratefully up at his father. Then he bent his head and carefully finished painting the black nose on one of the dogs. A little touch of white paint on each nose made them look wet and shiny.

He stood back to admire his work and then, satisfied that he had done a good job he washed the brushes and put the tops on the paint. He called goodbye to his father and ran as fast as he could to Matt's house to find out what he would need to pack for his trip to Lystra.

Chapter twenty-one

Alex and Matt sat in the back of the carriage holding tightly onto Jonas' case. It contained the precious stones which Jonas was carrying to his customer in Lystra. Jonas sat in front of them in deep conversation with two other passengers. There were about five carriages like theirs, all being pulled by mules.

"There's safety in numbers," Jonas told them. "Travellers who go along these roads alone can get held up by robbers and there are also wild animals in some parts. If there are lots of people travelling together they're less likely to attack."

"I hope we see a lion," Alex said to his friend, "or a bear. That would be exciting!"

"Well I hope we don't," Matt replied, "I want to get to Lystra in one piece."

For several days the boys had enjoyed being carried along watching the miles roll past. Along the way they had filled up their water skins with water from the little streams or at the wells beside the road. When they came to a village they stocked up on food. Some nights they slept in a wayside inn and on others they wrapped themselves in their cloaks and slept on the ground.

The scenery was breath-taking. All around were mountains, valleys, woods and rivers all set against a blue, blue sky. Who would want to live in a cold country? Alex thought as he watched the sunlight glistening on the little stream than ran alongside the path. He laughed at a white stork standing in the shallows of a river watching for a fish to swim near enough for him to catch for his dinner. As they passed a clump of chestnut trees a startled deer ran past them to disappear into the wood.

Suddenly, the carriage stopped dead and the boys were almost thrown from their seats.

"What's happening?" Matt asked.

"It's a wild boar on the road up ahead," Jonas replied, "Hopefully, it will just move off. It's a fully grown male and looks pretty bad tempered. Fortunately, we saw it before we got too close. If they're cornered they will attack and their tusks are vicious."

Alex craned his head round the side of the carriage and saw the huge beast with mean looking little eyes and two white tusks coming from its bottom jaw. "Wow!" he said softly, "he's cool!"

Slowly, the animal turned around and after looking at the mules standing frozen with fear up ahead, he calmly walked off the road and down a narrow path before disappearing into the trees.

"Phew!" Matt said, "That was a bit too cool for me. I'm glad he's gone."

Cautiously, the carriage driver moved the mules forward and everyone breathed a sigh of relief as they continued once more on their journey.

"How long before we arrive?" Matt asked his father after they had gone a few more miles without incident.

Jonas turned to look at the boys in the back, "Not long now," he smiled, "if we don't meet too many wild animals we should be in Lystra by night fall."

"Good," Alex said. "My back is getting sore bumping up and down on this hard seat."

Jonas was right. It was just beginning to get dark as they saw the road start to climb up ahead. At the top of the mound were the city walls. The fields around them were green and well-watered and there was a stream flowing around the outside of the walls. To one side of the road they could see a large temple and the splendid statue of a god at the entrance.

"Which god is that?" Matt asked. Alex peered out of the carriage to look. "It looks like a temple to Zeus," he said, "but the statue is of Hermes—you can see that because of the wings on his shoes and his cap."

"Two gods in one temple?" Matt said in surprise, "How does that work?"

Alex laughed, "Well," he explained, "Hermes is supposed to be the messenger of the gods, so I expect the statue of Hermes is in honour of Zeus who is said to be the king of the gods."

"Actually," Jonas said, joining in the conversation, "there's a legend about Zeus and Hermes. It was said that they once came here in disguise. No one would give them hospitality apart from two old peasants. The gods were very angry so they wiped out the whole population and only saved the two peasants. These two took care of a splendid temple and were turned into two great trees when they died. The people here still believe this story."

Slowly, the carriage moved past the temple and through the city gates before drawing into the compound. In front of them was a large, flat roofed, single storey building made from large bricks with just one door and a few narrow windows.

"Lystra Inn!" shouted one of the carriage drivers. "We've arrived."

Gratefully, the boys climbed down from their seats in the carriage. They stood stretching their stiff bodies as their bags were taken from the carriage and into the inn.

"Food and bed," Jonas announced and led the way into the inn where there was a dining area and several bowls of bread, olives, eggs, nuts and porridge laid out on a low table with eating mats spread around it.

"We'll put our beds out on the roof tonight," Jonas said after they had eaten all they could, "it's too hot to sleep inside. Tomorrow you can explore Lystra while I see my customer. Then we'll see if we can catch up with Barnabas and Paul."

Chapter twenty-two

Matt and Alex were tired after their journey and by the time they got up next morning Jonas had already left to meet his customer who wanted to buy the jewels. Jonas had left a message with the innkeeper to say he would meet the boys later in the day in the market place.

After a good breakfast the two boys left the inn, blinking as they came out into the bright sunshine.

"Right," announced Matt, "we need to be organised. We mustn't just wander about looking for Irana."

Alex who was already hurrying down the road towards the centre of the city in his impatience stopped and looked back at his friend. "Ok," he agreed, "so what's the plan?"

"We visit the main temples of the various gods," Matt said, "and we go to the large houses where Romans might employ fortune tellers or ..." he hesitated.

"Or ...?" Alex asked, "Sorcerers? Witches? Devil worshippers? Is that what you were going to say Matt?"

Matt hung his head, "Sorry Alex," he said, "I hate to think of Irana as any of those too. But those are the people we need to look for if we're going to find her."

Alex sighed, "You're right. Come on then, where's the first stop?"

For the rest of the morning the two friends called in on all the large houses around the city asking if anyone knew of a fortune teller with bright red hair who might be employed by a wealthy Roman. It wasn't quite so easy searching here because many of the people spoke a different language. But as all the schools in the Roman Empire taught Latin, the boys were able to find educated people who understood them. At one house they were able to talk to a fortune teller who offered to call up a spirit of the dead to ask for help in the search. They refused her help and left hastily, although Alex had for a moment been tempted to agree.

After they had visited all the large houses they stopped at a roadside stall for a rest. They enjoyed a drink of fresh milk and a hunk of bread with cheese.

"Where to now?" Alex asked at last.

"The temples," Matt replied and rather reluctantly they left their cool spot under the canopy of the stall and continued their search. There were many small wayside shrines, but the boys by now realised that fortune tellers and magicians were usually to be found in the larger temple areas where the more wealthy people went. It cost money to have your fortune told. So, it was there they concentrated their search.

They walked back outside the city gates to the temple of Zeus they had seen earlier. Inside the temple area was a grove of trees and a spring of water where people gathered. There were one or two people there who were considered 'holy'. They were dressed in bright robes and people were paying them money to pray to the gods for success or to heal someone who was ill. Alex and Matt spent some time there asking for news of Irana but no one had seen her.

From here they continued on to other temples in Lystra. The number of temples seemed endless but they were determined. If Irana was in Lystra they were going to find her.

"There are so many different gods!" Matt exclaimed at last as they collapsed exhausted beside the path. "We've been to temples to Dionysus, Apollo, Artemis and Poseidon. How many more gods are there?"

"Loads more," Alex said, "but I think we've visited all the main temples in Lystra. Irana isn't here is she Matt?"

Matt shook his head, "I don't think she is. I'm sorry, Alex."

Alex sighed, "Come on," he said at last, "let's rest for a while and then go to meet your father."

It was now the middle of the afternoon and after a doze in the shade the boys made their way towards the market place where they had agreed to meet Jonas. The heat of the day was fading and other people were beginning to come out of their homes.

The market was already crowded when they arrived. Jonas was standing impatiently waiting for them at the entrance. "Come on you two," he said excitedly, "Paul and Barnabas are here preaching to a huge crowd. There are already a few people in Lystra who have become followers of Jesus."

Quickening their pace Alex and Matt followed Jonas into the middle of the market place where Paul was standing on some steps and telling the crowd the good news about Jesus.

Chapter twenty-three

Jonas and the boys pushed nearer to the front so that they could see more clearly. It was amazing how the people were listening so intently. This message was very different from the stories of the gods these people had heard about since they were small. This God was alive! It seemed that he cared about them. This was something completely new. Their gods were cruel and selfish, but this God had died so that they could live.

Alex noticed that there was one man who was sitting very close to Paul who hadn't moved. He was staring at Paul and hanging onto his every word. Alex could see that he couldn't walk. His feet were at a funny angle and were very thin. But his face showed that he believed everything Paul was saying.

It seemed Paul had noticed the man too, because at that moment he looked directly at him. The next thing he did was to call out to the man, "Stand up on your feet!"

Straight away the man stood up and started to walk! His feet looked perfectly normal.

A gasp went round the crowd. How could a man who had never walked before suddenly get up and walk? The people all started shouting at once and then it became a chant.

"What are they shouting?" Alex asked.

Jonas shook his head, "They're speaking Lycaonian," he said, "I've no idea what they're saying." Jonas turned to a man next to him who was watching what was going on. "What are they shouting?" he called to the man.

"They're saying that the gods have come down to us in human form," the man shouted back. "They are calling the quiet one Zeus and the one who is speaking, Hermes."

The next thing that happened was that the local priest, whose temple to Zeus they had visited only that morning, arrived. He came leading several huge bulls wearing wreaths round their necks and Alex suddenly knew what was happening as he'd seen it before. "They want to take Paul and Barnabas to the temple. They plan to sacrifice the animals as an offering to them like they do to the gods," he gasped.

"It must be because of the legend," Matt exclaimed. "They think the gods have come in disguise again and don't want to make the mistake and be destroyed like the people in the legend."

"You're right, Matt," Jonas agreed, "but whatever will Paul and Barnabas do now?"

By this time Barnabas and Paul had also realised what was happening and were very upset. They tore their clothes and rushed into the crowd, "Men!" they shouted, "Why are you doing this? We're human just like you. We just want to tell you about the living God who made heaven and earth and sea and everything in them. He gives rain from heaven and provides you with food and fills your hearts with joy."

It seemed to take ages for the crowd to calm down. They were sure Paul and Barnabas were gods and kept trying to sacrifice to them. The man who had been healed had somehow got lost in the crowd. Meanwhile the bulls were getting angry with all the noise and were eventually led away by the priest.

"Phew!" Matt said at last. "That was a bit close."

"Yes," agreed Alex, "I wonder if the people realise now that it was God and not Paul and Barnabas who healed the man?"

"Maybe a few do," Jonas said, "but I think most of the people are confused." He paused, looking over their shoulders to another crowd gathering on the other side of the market place. "And I don't like the look of those men over there either," he went on, "they're not from Lystra and they look as if they're up to no good. Stay together boys, I'm going over to find out."

Chapter twenty-four

Matt and Alex tried hard to keep up with Jonas as he shouldered his way through the crowd to get to the group he had spotted. As they got closer they could hear bits of the conversation. "We've come from Iconium to warn you," the men were saying to the people. "This Paul is a trouble maker. He caused a lot of problems in our city. You need to get rid of him quickly."

It was hard to believe the change in the people. Only minutes earlier they had been trying to worship Paul and now they were deciding that he should be killed. A few of them started to pick up stones and move towards Paul and Barnabas.

Paul and Barnabas were still trying to speak to the crowd on the other side and didn't hear what was going on. Barnabas was talking to one group and Paul was arguing with another.

"Quick," hissed Alex to Matt, "we need to go and warn Paul and Barnabas to hide."

They pushed through the crowd as quickly as they could, desperately elbowing people out of the way as they went. But it was too late. The anger and hatred had moved across the crowd more quickly than their feet. By the time they reached Paul they saw the men throwing huge stones at him.

"No," shouted Jonas in despair, but his voice was lost in the shouts of "Kill him, kill him!" coming from the crowd. Huge stones were being hurled at him from all directions. Alex and Matt watched in horror as Paul staggered and then fell to the ground, the stones rattling around him as he fell.

"Where's Barnabas?" Matt whispered anxiously, "I can't see him."

"I hope he's hiding somewhere," Alex replied.

At last the stone throwing stopped. "I think he's dead," Jonas said in horror, "Look they're going to throw his body out of the city." They watched as the men took hold of Paul's body and dragged him along the ground through the market place towards the city gates.

A few people silently followed at a distance. Jonas, Alex and Matt joined the silent procession following the body of Paul as it was pulled over the rocky ground. Once outside of the city the men dumped the body on the road. They brushed the dirt off their hands and without a backward glance walked back into the city.

Alex and Matt stood with the others looking down at the broken body of Paul. The last time Alex had felt as miserable as this was when Irana had been kidnapped.

Then quite suddenly, everything changed. There was no dramatic voice or light from heaven but as the watchers stood they saw the body move. Then before all their eyes Paul stood up. No one spoke. Without a word he walked calmly back through the city gates and into the city.

Alex and the others followed behind. His heart was beating fast. Once again he had seen how great and powerful God was. This God was the one he was trusting in. This was the God who Paul had said was kind and good.

At that moment he was sure. One day he was going to find his sister.

Chapter twenty-five

The three travellers were not far now from Antioch. After the dramatic events in Lystra, Paul and Barnabas had left the following morning and were travelling on to Derbe. As Jonas had finished his business they too decided to return home.

The journey seemed shorter on the way back perhaps because they had slept some of the way. There had been no incidents with wild boars and Alex hadn't seen a lion although he had watched out for one as they came through the forest area where they were said to live.

"I will be glad to be home," Jonas sighed, "travelling is so tiring. I don't know how Paul and Barnabas manage it, especially as they often walk from one place to the next."

"And they regularly get beaten and stoned so they're not exactly in the best of health," Matt agreed.

"Why is it?" Alex wondered, "why is it that wherever Paul goes to preach there seems to be trouble?"

"There are a few reasons I suppose," Jonas said.

"One is that people don't like being told they're believing the wrong things and trusting in the wrong gods," Matt said.

"That's one reason I'm sure," Jonas said, "another is the evil one, who we call the devil, is busy trying to turn people away from the truth."

"It makes you wonder why Paul carries on," Alex said.

Jonas smiled, "Paul believes the truth is worth dying for. He says we have to go through hardships to be part of the kingdom of God," he explained, "think how wonderful it is when people realise that there is a God who really loves them and not all the frightening gods they've been taught about before."

The mules were slowing up at last and the travellers could see they were beginning to walk more carefully along the road that led between the houses leading to Alex's home.

As they arrived they saw Sophia and Julia sitting outside the house drinking a glass of wine. They jumped up when they saw the mule cart and hurried to help the boys down.

Jonas greeted his wife and then went into the workshop to say hallo to Kostas.

"How was it?" Sophia asked the boys anxiously, "Did you see or hear anything?"

Alex hugged his mother, "If you mean did I see or hear anything about Irana, no, nothing at all," he said sadly.

Sophia's shoulders drooped, "We have been praying since you went that you would hear some news of her," she sighed.

Julia put her arm round her friend, "I am sorry, Sophia," she said, "but we mustn't give up. God knows where she is."

"I wish he'd tell us then," Alex said impatiently.

"But we do know where she isn't," Matt encouraged his friend, "She's not in Jerusalem, Cyprus, Perga or Lystra. There are two other places we've got to search—Neapolis and Rome."

"Surely not," Julia exclaimed, "Neapolis is a huge area and Rome is miles away."

Alex shrugged. "If I have to go all the way to Rome, then I will," he said in a determined voice.

Julia looked doubtful. "Jonas rarely travels into Neapolis on business," she said, "and none of us have ever been to Rome. I really don't know…" her voice trailed off.

"Oh no, Alex, it's too far," Sophia groaned running both hands through her hair in despair.

Matt straightened his shoulders, "I know one way we might be able to travel further," he said slowly looking hard at Alex.

"How?" Alex asked eagerly.

"With the junior sports team!" Matt said. "You will just have to practise and practise so that you get chosen to represent Antioch in the pentathlon team. Your javelin throwing is already good enough so you'll just need to practise discus and long jump. But you can do that," he continued confidently.

"You're right," Alex agreed, "The sports team travel right across to Delphi and Corinth and even to Olympia. If I can get into the team they will take me all over the Roman Empire. Thanks, Matt! That's what I will do!"

The two women sighed. They could see the boys were determined to go ahead with this crazy plan.

Chapter twenty-six

Alex put the plan into action straight away. He went regularly to the gymnasium for training in long jump and discus throwing and at the same time continued to practice his javelin technique, with Matt's help.

As the days and weeks went by his standard improved and the trainers at the gymnasium were very pleased with his progress.

"I'd like to represent Antioch in the junior pentathlon," he told Leo, his personal trainer, one day.

"Well!" Leo replied, "Your javelin throwing is already up to standard and your discus and long jump are almost good enough too. We're planning a tour to Macedonia and Achaia and will be having competitions in a few towns before arriving in time for the Athens games. We leave in three weeks. You should get on that trip if you carry on improving."

Alex rushed from the gymnasium to Matt's house to share the news.

"The ship will take us to Neapolis. I'll be travelling in the area where Irana might have been taken," Alex told him. "Leo will be with the team to arrange for our accommodation and food and stuff. And the Antioch games committee pay for my boat fare and everything. It's amazing!"

Matt tried very hard to be happy for his friend. But he also knew that he wouldn't be on the trip with Alex. Alex saw his friend's face.

"Oh Matt," he said, "Is there no way you could come too? I don't really want to go alone."

"I don't think so," Matt answered looking ruefully down at his thin legs, "I won't ever be an athlete. But you will have the other lads with you and Leo will take good care of everything."

"I suppose so," Alex said rather uncertainly.

"Of course so," Matt replied, "You must go, it's your big opportunity. And think how fantastic it will be to represent Antioch at the games!"

Alex brightened, "You're right," he said, "and anyway I may not improve enough to be chosen so it's not worth worrying about at the moment."

They sat together under the eucalyptus tree for a while, each with his own thoughts. In the background they could hear the men who had gathered in Jonas' house for a meeting. Every now and then the voices were raised and then they would go quiet again.

"What are they discussing today?" Alex asked.

Matt looked embarrassed for a moment and then said, "They're discussing whether Greeks should become Jews before they can be saved by Jesus."

"What?" Alex said surprised, "I've not heard that before. I thought when we became Christians we were all the same. Who says we have to become Jews?"

"Oh some men who've come down from Judea," Matt replied, "The argument's been going on for several days.

They say that Greek Christians should obey the old
Jewish laws."

"I don't like the sound of that." Alex said, "What do
Barnabas and Paul say about it? They're back from their
travels aren't they?"

Matt nodded, "Oh yes, they came back a few weeks
ago. And they had quite an argument with the men. Your
father and mine suggested they go to Jerusalem with a
few other church members to ask the apostles and church
leaders there what they think about it. I hope they'll come
back soon with an answer. It's all very confusing."

Chapter twenty-seven

Sophia was not quite as enthusiastic as Alex when she heard that he had been accepted to represent Antioch on the athletics trip. "Alex is so impulsive," she said to Kostas, "I'd be happier if he had Matt with him."

Kostas agreed, "Maybe I'll have a word with Jonas and Leo and see what can be arranged," he said. "After all, they must take boys with them to help with practising and Matt knows all the rules of the games."

The next day, Kostas went down to the gymnasium and spoke to Leo. Alex was over the moon when Leo agreed to the suggestion. "I will need a few extra lads to help," he said, "and I know Matt is a hard worker."

"Now that you're coming with us everything will be fine," Alex told his friend excitedly when the two families met together that evening for a meal.

After they had eaten Alex and Matt spread out a map and followed with their fingers all the places they would be visiting. Sophia and Julia were anxiously discussing what the boys would need to take for the trip and Jonas and Kostas were in deep conversation about the letter that Paul and Barnabas had brought back from Jerusalem.

"It seems that Peter agreed with Paul." Jonas was telling Kostas, "He reminded the council at Jerusalem that we don't have to follow rules to be forgiven. Jesus did everything when he died for us. I think there was quite a long discussion but they all came to the same decision."

"That's a relief," Kostas said, "I have nothing against Jews," he went on, smiling at Jonas, "my best friend is a Jew. But I don't particularly want to become one myself!"

Sophia and Julia had stopped their discussion and were listening in on the conversation. "So what does the letter say?" Julia asked.

"Well!" Jonas replied, "It says that Greeks don't have to follow all the Jewish rules. The only thing it says is that Christians shouldn't eat food offered to idols. Also they should make sure the meat they eat has been properly drained of blood. Otherwise, nothing else."

Sophia sighed, "I'm very glad about that," she said. "Now I hope we'll stop all this silly arguing about things."

Julia smiled a little sadly. "Unfortunately, we will always find something to argue about. Being a Christian doesn't make us perfect."

"You're right Julia," Jonas said, "even Paul and Barnabas have had a disagreement. It seems Barnabas wants to take Mark on their next journey but Paul won't have him."

"Why ever not?" Sophia asked.

"I expect it's because Mark left Paul and Barnabas on their first journey," Alex said, "Do you remember, Matt?"

"Yes, I remember," Matt answered. "Paul was pretty mad about that."

"Barnabas is more gentle than Paul, I suppose," Julia said, "It can't be easy keeping up with Paul's high standard."

"So what's going to happen now?" Sophia asked.

Jonas smiled, "They've decided that Barnabas will take Mark and Paul will ask his friend Silas to go with him. There will be two different journeys to spread the good news about Jesus now. Isn't it good that God can even use our mistakes so that something good comes out of it?"

"So, everyone is going on journeys!" Matt said, "Barnabas and Mark are going to Cyprus, Paul and Silas are going overland to Derbe and Lystra and then on to Troas and we're going the furthest by ship, to Neapolis!"

"And, maybe on this trip we will find Irana and she can watch me win the pentathlon event," Alex said.

Chapter twenty-eight

The junior athletic team had been on the ship for what seemed weeks. After saying goodbye to their families at Seleucia they had eagerly scrambled on deck and settled into their cabins for the long sail to Neapolis. There were twenty of them altogether, plus a few helpers. Matt and Alex shared a small cabin with four other boys. During the day they did exercises on deck to keep fit and at night they settled into their narrow bunks and discussed the competitions ahead.

The winds were mostly favourable as the ship ploughed its way through the waters day after day. There were a couple of days when the wind dropped and the sails hung lifeless from the mast and they made very little progress. On other days the wind blew strongly and they seemed to dance effortlessly over the waves.

It felt as if they were sailing off the edge of the world, as hour after hour went by, surrounded by nothing but water. Now and then they would pass pretty little islands where turtles swam close to the beaches. Once they saw a school of dolphins swimming nearby and leaping out of the water in sheer joy. And on another occasion they saw a great white shark swimming rather too close to the ship than was comfortable.

Finally, they could see land. What a welcome sight it was. The boys stood at the ship's rail and watched as Neapolis grew larger and larger.

"Here we are, Neapolis!" The captain announced, "Stand back everyone while we dock." The crew brought the ship carefully alongside the quay. It was a large vessel and didn't stop easily, but with great skill they moored with hardly a bump.

"Passengers off quickly!" the captain shouted. "We have all this cargo to unload and another lot to take on board before lunch time."

Hastily the athletes jumped ashore, staggering a little as they felt the firm ground beneath their feet. "Wow, I do feel strange," Matt said.

"Yes," agreed Alex, "my legs feel all wobbly after being on the boat for so long."

Leo was busy organising the team. He had hired six pack horses to carry all their equipment which was already being loaded onto them. "Hurry up lads," he said, "we have a ten mile walk to Philippi. We want to get there before dark."

"Ten miles!" groaned one of the boys, "I'm exhausted already. Can't we use the horses?"

"Certainly not, they're already loaded down," Leo said firmly, "And you have two days to get fit before the competition in Philippi so the walk will help to build up your stamina."

"At least it's a good road." Alex remarked as they set off down the wide track covered in large flat stones that had been carefully fitted together to make a smooth surface.

"Yes," Matt said, "It's called Via Egnatia. The Romans built it about 250 years ago to make it easier for them to get from one Roman colony to another. It's almost 700 miles long!"

Alex stopped and looked down at his friend in amazement, "Where did you learn all this stuff?" he asked Matt.

Matt laughed and went red with embarrassment, "My father told me," he explained, "I'm really interested in Roman history. A bit strange I suppose."

"I don't know how you keep all those facts and figures in your head," Alex said with a sigh, "I'm hopeless at brain work."

As they talked, the miles rolled by. One stretch of the road was hard work as it rose over some hills before going down again onto the Macedonian plain. As the weary travellers approached Philippi the light was already beginning to fade.

Ahead was a grand sight. They could see the city walls and the square watch towers placed at intervals along them. As they trudged through the gates the road led into a cool grove with shrubs and fountains. They stopped for a drink and then continued along the main street towards the centre of Philippi.

As they walked they were amazed by the huge monuments and statues made of wood, marble and metal. Some were covered in precious stones and others gilded in gold that reflected the pink of the setting sun.

"Phew! Look at all that gold and silver!" Alex exclaimed staring up at a particularly grand statue of the Roman Emperor.

"Yes," Matt agreed, "Philippi is a very wealthy city. It's because of all the gold and silver mines in the mountains round here. The Romans have spent a lot of money on this colony over the years. It's like a miniature Rome."

"This is the gymnasium," Leo told the boys as they walked alongside a high stone wall. They paused at the gate and peered in. It looked very grand with stone pillars and statues of Roman gods also decorated with gold and silver. "Beyond this entrance is a courtyard where the athletics take place." Leo went on, "It also has two large sports fields and baths and even a library. Tomorrow we'll go there to practice ready for the games."

The weary group continued a little further into the city and at last Leo said, "Here we are. This is the inn where we are staying." Thankfully, the boys walked the last few steps into the dining area where they were given a welcome meal of bread, cheese, fruit and a jug of watery wine to drink.

"And now, to bed," Leo told the boys and none of them argued. They were all happy to take off their sandals, settle down onto their beds and fall into a deep sleep.

Chapter twenty-nine

The following morning was spent at the gymnasium. All the boys were keen to get as much practice as possible before the competition the next day. This would be a good warm up for the important games at Athens at the end of their tour. Alex had grown taller in the last few weeks and his long jump had greatly improved. He was one of the best in the team. Leo had high hopes that all the boys would do well on the tour.

After the practice Leo gathered the athletes together for a talk to give them last minute instructions. Matt wasn't needed for this so he was glad to sit in the cool library and look at some of the wonderful books and maps that were there. There were books about the various Greek and Roman gods which he flicked through. He was a Jew and knew there was only one God so had little interest in them. He found one on the history of Philippi and happily sat down to read all about Philip II of Macedonia who the city was named after.

He was interrupted by Leo calling him, "Come on, you book worm! It's time to go back to the inn for lunch," he laughed. Reluctantly, Matt put his book back on the shelf and joined Alex and the others.

Alex was unusually quiet on the walk back to the inn. Matt was happy not to talk. His head was still full of how

Philip had discovered the gold in the mountains and set up
the city. But when they were eating their meal of freshly
baked bread and soup, Matt noticed Alex had hardly
touched his. "You're not eating much Alex," he remarked.

"No," mumbled Alex, "I'm not very hungry."

"What's up?" Matt enquired, looking at his friend's
white face. "Are you ill?"

Alex shook his head. "Not ill, just very worried," he said
to his friend. "We need to talk. Can we find somewhere
quiet?"

"Sure." Matt agreed looking anxiously at his friend. He
hastily finished his soup and bread and the two of them
went outside and found some shade under a fig tree where
they sat down together. "Well?" Matt asked, "What is it?"

"I can't do it, Matt." He burst out, "Whatever shall we do?"

"What do you mean?" Matt asked, "What can't you do?"

"The games—I can't compete in them." Alex said.

"It's not like you to have nerves." Matt said surprised.

"No you don't understand. It's not nerves. I just can't. It
wouldn't be right."

"Alex," Matt said again, "You're not making any sense."

Alex sighed deeply, "Leo gave us instructions today
about the games," he said, wiping his hands across his
eyes, "We have to make an offering of food to Zeus at the
opening ceremony. I'm a Christian, Matt. I can't do that."

"But," Matt said, "can't you just stand to one side and
let the others do that bit? That's what you did at the
Antioch games."

"Yes, but this time it's different," Alex said, "Each of
us has to separately give an offering and take an oath in
front of the statue of Zeus. It would be wrong to do that

wouldn't it? How can I expect God to help me find Irana if I worship Zeus?"

Matt nodded. He was quiet for a long time. "So, what are you going to do?" he asked at last.

"I'm going to have to tell Leo," Alex replied miserably, "I don't know what will happen."

"What are you going to have to tell Leo?" a voice asked and the boys jumped guiltily as they turned to see Leo standing there looking down at them.

Hesitantly, Alex explained to Leo his problem, "I didn't realize I was going to have to make an oath to Zeus," he said.

"Don't worry about it," Leo said kindly, "it doesn't matter if you believe in Zeus or not. All you have to do is say the oath and bow to the statue. It's just a tradition. Lots of the other boys don't believe either."

"I can't do it. I'm a Christian," Alex said.

"You know you could win the pentathlon, don't you?" Leo said persuasively, "Is it worth giving up the prize for this Jesus? Think of how proud your parents and friends back home will be?"

"I can't," Alex said again. "I can't bow down to an idol."

Leo wasn't a bad man but he was beginning to lose patience. "It's up to you," he said, "You can't enter the competition without making the oath in front of Zeus. Either you do it or you'll have to return to Antioch. I can't keep you on the team if you're not willing to participate. Think about it."

"I've thought about it all morning," Alex said again looking down at the ground, "but my mind is made up. I'm pulling out of the team."

"You don't know what you're saying boy," Leo said, "You can't just pull out."

"I must," Alex said, "I'm so sorry to let you down."

Leo shook his head. "Then you're a young fool!" he said.

Chapter thirty

The next morning all the athletes were in high spirits as they ate their breakfast ready for the games. Leo was giving them last minute instructions. "Meet outside in five minutes," he said, "and we'll go together to the gymnasium."

While all the other boys went up to their rooms to collect their equipment and fill their water skins for the day, Alex and Matt remained at the breakfast table.

Leo gave them a glance at the door. "Changed your mind?" he asked Alex, who shook his head. "Well!" Leo said shortly, "when we leave Philippi tomorrow you're on your own." With that he was gone, leaving them alone.

The two boys sat for a while thinking their own thoughts. Then Matt spoke firmly, "Right, let's go."

"Go?" Alex asked, "Go where?"

Matt smiled, "Don't forget why we're here," he said practically, "let's go and look round Philippi. We have all day to look for Irana. You heard what Leo said, after tonight we'll be on our own. Tomorrow we will need to go back to Neapolis and search for her there. Then we'll need to think how to get home."

Alex looked gratefully at his friend, "What would I do without you?" he asked.

"You would struggle," Matt agreed, pulling Alex up from the bench and dragging him into the sunshine.

It was a beautiful day and as they walked, Alex felt happier than he had for a long time. "I've made the right decision, you know," he told his friend.

"I know you have." Matt agreed, "I didn't realise how much idol worship there was in the games. But we're a bit stuck now. How much money do you have Alex?" he went on.

Alex searched in his pocket, "Not very much," he said counting out his coins, "just a few mites."

"I have one denarius," Matt said. "That should keep us going for a bit. Tonight we'll be able to eat at the inn and have a bed there, so we don't have to worry until tomorrow."

Matt and Alex had arrived at the market place and began asking at the stalls if anyone had seen a fortune teller with flaming red hair. As usual the people shook their heads. "Philippi is full of fortune tellers," they were told.

Towards lunchtime they stopped at a well to fill up their water skins and asked a woman there. "Oh yes. I've seen her," the woman said, "Ugly looking girl with scraggy red hair. She hangs around by the temples."

"Must be someone different," Matt said firmly, "You'd never call Irana ugly," and Alex agreed.

They continued asking for a while but apart from one or two others who had seen an ugly, thin girl with red hair, no one else could help, so they moved from the market place towards the area where there were temples to many different gods.

Alex sighed, "It's depressing round here, isn't it?" he said turning back to his friend. "I never realised it before but watching all these people ringing their bells and bowing and beating themselves, I can see how pointless it all is."

They came to a temple where people were worshipping in front of a steep flight of steps with a row of columns at the top, behind which was the statue of a goddess. Many were carrying a rose which they laid at the foot of the steps.

"Which god is this?" Matt asked.

"It's the goddess Aphrodite," Alex replied. "Do you remember her, Matt? She was the one who was supposed to have come out of the waves near Paphos?"

"Of course," Matt said, "that's the one the Romans call Venus."

"That's right," Alex said, "and some call her by the name of the Egyptian god, Isis."

Matt shivered, "And Agatha was a priestess of Isis, if I remember rightly."

As he spoke a small group had gathered at the foot of the steps near to where people had been laying roses. Curiously, the boys drew closer to the group. They appeared to be waiting for someone to speak. The boys moved round so that they could see what was going on. They both saw her at the same moment.

"It can't be!" gasped Matt.

"Oh no!" Alex whispered. All the colour left his face as he stared at the girl. She was ugly, very thin and her hair was filthy and unkempt.

But without a doubt it was Irana.

Alex and Matt were rooted to the spot. Neither knew what to say or do. They watched as in a strange toneless voice she told the man that his wife would give birth to a daughter. "Call her Irana," she told him and he kissed her outstretched hand in gratitude. She looked up and saw the two boys staring at her in horror, but there was no glimmer of recognition on her face. Then, an older woman took her arm and they moved away, disappearing into the crowd leaving the two boys staring after her.

They sat down on the steps where she had been. Both were shaking with shock and excitement. Their search was over. They had found Irana. But she looked dreadful. What had happened to her? And now they had found her, what could they do?

Chapter thirty-one

Matt recovered first. "We've found her Alex," he said, gripping his friend's arm. "We've found her at last!"

"Yes," Alex agreed, "But now what? She looks so weird and she didn't even recognize us."

Matt thought for a moment. "Ok, Alex," he said firmly, "the first thing we must do is get a letter to your family. And then we must make a plan."

The colour was slowly coming back into Alex's face and with the urging of his friend he went back with him to the inn. The athletes had not yet come back for which they were grateful. Alex used his mites to purchase a small parchment and they borrowed a pen from the inn keeper.

Matt took charge. He put his father's address on the top and wrote these words: "Tell Kostas we have found Irana at Philippi. Come quickly! She needs help. Matt and Alex." Quickly, they took the note to the city gate where they paid one denarius to the postman. The man was about to leave on horse-back and would take it to Neapolis. "It should catch the morning ship to Antioch," he assured them.

"That was all our money gone in one go," Matt sighed.

Alex nodded, "We'll survive," he told his friend. "We can find a place to sleep rough. We don't need a bed in an inn.

There are plenty of date and coconut palms by the river. And we can catch fish."

"This is your kind of adventure, Alex, not mine," Matt said with a weak smile.

Alex was beginning to get over the shock of seeing his sister in such a terrible state. "What can we do now?" he asked, "We could try to kidnap Irana back, but then what?"

"Then," Matt said, putting his hand to his eye, "they'd give me another black eye. And they might break your leg this time."

Alex nodded miserably. "You're right," he agreed, "so what can we do?"

"First we need to pray," Matt said, "We have no money and are a long way from home. Then we need to check on Irana each day and not raise any suspicions. It's probably best she doesn't see us. If she suddenly remembers us they may take her away and hide her. We must wait until help comes."

"Do you know," Alex said suddenly, "If I had gone to the games I wouldn't have found Irana?"

"That's true," Matt said, "God's been with us today and we didn't know it!"

Together they wandered out of the city gate and down to the riverside. It was peaceful there.

"Let's sit here for a bit," Matt suggested.

"I could do with a rest and I don't want to go back to the inn just yet," Alex agreed dipping his hot feet into the river.

The gentle sound of the water over the stones and the occasional plop of a fish coming up to the surface to catch a fly, soothed them. Idly, they watched four men up river climbing down from the bank into the water.

"What's going on up there?" Alex wondered, "Perhaps they're catching fish."

Matt stood up, "Why don't we go and see?" he suggested and as they walked closer he said, "It looks like a meeting of some kind."

Alex agreed, "And if I'm not mistaken, that's Paul in the water."

"So it is! But who's with him? I don't recognise any of those people," Matt said.

"Yes, you do," said Alex. "One of them is that man who came from Jerusalem, Silas. I don't know who the other two men are."

They were close to the group now and could see that some women were also going into the water to join the men. "It's a baptism!" Matt exclaimed, "Those must be new Christians!"

They were just in time to watch the final woman being lowered into the water. Shyly they sat down at the edge of the group next to a woman who had obviously been baptised as she was soaking wet and was drying her hair with her shawl.

"Hallo," she greeted them, "You don't come from these parts do you?"

After they had explained who they were she told them her name was Ruth. She lived in the city and worked for the lady who was talking to Paul and Silas. "That's Lydia," the woman explained, "a very well-known business woman. She runs her own cloth business in Philippi. She uses the most expensive purple dye and is very wealthy.

And she has a huge house in town. The younger man there is Timothy who is travelling with them and the other man is Luke. He comes from these parts—he's a doctor."

Paul and Lydia were closer to them now. They could hear the conversation. "If you consider me a believer in the Lord," Lydia was saying, "come and stay at my house." They could hear Paul thanking her and agreeing to the suggestion.

Alex sighed. He wished someone would invite him to their home. They had no idea where they would stay tomorrow.

"We need to be going, Alex," Matt suddenly said, "Or we'll miss our supper."

Saying a hasty goodbye to their new friend, the two boys ran back to the inn as fast as they could. This might be their last good meal for a while, so they wanted to make the most of it.

Leo and the athletes were already sitting down eating when they arrived. They slipped onto a bench at the edge of the dining room and listened as the boys talked about their exciting day at the games. It seemed they had beaten the team from Philippi in running and boxing but the Lystra team had won the pentathlon. One or two of the boys looked sideways at Alex as they spoke and for a moment he felt disappointed. Matt kicked him under the table to remind him he had done the right thing and not bowed down to an idol and they had found Irana! Alex grinned at his friend.

At the end of the meal Leo came over to them and pushed a packet across the table towards them. "That's your fare home," he said gruffly, "Try to keep safe," and with that he turned away. "Everyone to bed!" he shouted. "We have an early start in the morning." Alex and Matt picked up the precious parcel and found enough money there for them to survive for several weeks. God hadn't forgotten them.

Alex looked down at the money. He didn't know what was going to happen next. But he did know that God was great and good and that he cared. He would trust God, whatever happened.

Chapter thirty-two

Over the next few days Alex and Matt had a routine. They had found a good place to sleep down by the river, near to where the Christians met to pray. Fortunately, they had their sleeping mats with them so were able to keep warm. Every morning they got up, washed in the river then went to the market to buy food for the day. They then spent the rest of the morning sitting at the temple of Aphrodite watching Irana. In the afternoon they would go to the place of prayer to listen to Paul and Silas talking about Jesus.

Several times they saw Paul and Silas leaving Lydia's home and walking down to the riverside, so they would follow a little way behind. Other people were following too wanting to hear their teaching. One girl was always there. She was a slave girl like Irana who was able to tell the future and her owners seemed to be making a great deal of money from her. Every day she shouted the same thing. "These men are servants of the Most High God, who are telling you the way to be saved." Paul and Silas never took any notice of her but carried on walking as if they'd not heard.

"Do you think Paul will strike her blind like he did Elymas?" Alex asked his friend sadly. "Do you remember when we were in Cyprus Paul told him 'the hand of the

Lord is against you'? I wonder if people like her and Irana can ever be made normal again."

They often saw Ruth at the riverside, the woman they had spoken to on their first visit. She sometimes looked at them curiously but she never asked why they were so far from home. They were glad, as they didn't want to say too much to anyone about why they were in Philippi. It was safer that way. The people who held Irana must never suspect that they were being watched.

After they had been in Philippi for a week the boys got into the habit of going to the city gate in the late afternoon to wait for the party travelling up from Neapolis. "It will take days for them to come," Alex said, "but I'm sure they will, as soon as they get our letter."

"I hope they come soon," Matt said, "I hate watching Irana every day and not being able to do anything to help."

The same woman was always with Irana at the temple and it was clear the girl was her slave. If she walked too slowly or if she stumbled the woman would cruelly shove her forward. Alex found it very difficult to watch without rushing to her defence.

They didn't go too close unless she went into a trance which she sometimes did when trying to get a message from the spirits for a customer. Then they would creep a little closer and listen to the strange messages that came from her.

When the woman took Irana away at the end of the morning the boys tried to follow to see where they went but because they didn't want to get too close they never managed to see where they could have gone.

On one particular day as they watched Irana being taken away they were interrupted by the sound of the slave girl shouting, "These men are servants of the Most High God, who are telling you the way to be saved."

"I think Paul and Silas must be fed up with that girl following them every day," Alex said as the boys caught up with the group going down to the riverside.

"I should think so," Matt agreed, "in fact, it looks as if he's going to speak to her." They saw Paul stop and turn round to look at the girl. The group of people walking with him stopped too and everyone waited to see what would happen next.

Then Paul spoke, only, he didn't appear to be talking to the girl. He seemed to be speaking to the spirit inside her. He said in a stern loud voice, "In the name of Jesus Christ I command you to come out of her!"

Instantly, the girl was still. She looked quite different. It was obvious from her face that the evil spirit had gone. The mad look in her eyes disappeared and her face looked perfectly calm. It was amazing.

Suddenly, there was confusion all around. The owners of the slave girl could see the change too. Her power to call up evil spirits had gone. They had made a lot of money from her and now they had lost their hope of getting even richer. Furiously, they grabbed hold of Paul and Silas and dragged them off to the market place to bring them before the magistrates.

In a daze Alex watched as Paul and Silas were dragged away. Alex turned to look at Matt his face alight with happiness. "Oh Matt!" he said, "It is possible! If that girl could be made well, then so can Irana!"

Matt nodded, "But the people who can do it are on their way to prison," he said dryly.

"Come on, Matt," Alex said, "We need to find out where they're taking them."

Hastily, the boys ran to the market place in time to hear the accusations being put to the magistrates. "These men are Jews and are throwing our city into an uproar by teaching things that are against Roman law," they heard the men saying.

By this time the crowd had joined in and were saying all kinds of lies. The magistrates ordered them to be stripped and beaten and to the boys' horror they watched as Paul and Silas were severely flogged. The jailer was called and told to throw them in prison and guard them carefully in an inner cell with their feet in the stocks.

"I don't feel like sleeping, tonight," Alex said. "Let's go to the prison and see if anything is happening there."

Chapter thirty-three

It was about midnight as they approached the prison. They could hear singing. "I recognise that song," Matt said, "It's one of the hymns we sing at the church in Antioch."

"It's Paul and Silas singing!" Alex said in amazement, "You'd think after being beaten they wouldn't have the energy. Now they're praying," he observed after the singing had stopped, "You can hear them quite clearly even from outside."

Suddenly, the ground began to move. "Hold on Alex," Matt said reaching out and grabbing Alex arm, "Feels like an earthquake." The boys were used to earthquakes as they had them sometimes in Antioch, but this one was more severe.

Alex and Matt were thrown down as the ground around them jerked and rose violently under their feet. At the same time the prison doors flew open and they could hear all the chains which held the prisoners breaking loose from their fixings. Then, as suddenly as the earthquake started it stopped. The boys waited to see if all the prisoners would run out of the doors into freedom. But it didn't happen. They watched as the jailer came out of his room next to the prison to see all the doors open.

"He must think all the prisoners have gone and knows he'll be in real trouble if they have," Alex said, as they saw him pull out his sword as if to kill himself.

"Don't harm yourself," Paul shouted from inside the prison, "We are all here!"

Trembling, the jailer called for some lights and rushed into the prison. The next thing Alex and Matt saw was the jailer bringing Paul and Silas out of prison and falling in front of them, "Men, what must I do to be saved?" they heard him say.

"Believe in the Lord Jesus," Paul and Silas replied, "and you will be saved—you and your household." By this time all the members of the jailer's household were out of bed and gathered round Paul and Silas listening as they told them the good news about Jesus. The jailer washed their wounds and then they all went to a pool nearby finding their way in the dark with only an oil lamp and the light of the moon to lead them. Alex and Matt watched from a distance as all the members of the household were baptised.

After that Paul and Silas came back to the jailer's house for a meal. The door was shut behind them and Alex and Matt were unable to hear any more.

"We might as well sleep here round the side of the prison," Alex said wearily, "It's a warm night and I'm suddenly very tired."

It seemed that they had hardly gone off to sleep when they were woken up by the sound of voices. It was only just getting light. Two officials were knocking on the jailer's door. "Release those men," they told him. Alex and Matt rubbed the sleep from their eyes as the jailer hurried to tell the news to Paul. "The magistrates have ordered that you and Silas be released. You can leave!"

Then they heard Paul's reply to the officers, "They beat us publicly without a trial, even though we are Roman citizens and threw us into prison. And now do they want to get rid of us quietly? No! Let them come themselves and escort us out."

"Good for him," said Alex as the officials, looking very worried, hurried off.

"I wonder what the magistrates will do now," Matt replied. "Let's wait and see."

They only had to wait a short while. Very soon they heard a group of men coming towards the prison. They saw them going in to the room where Paul and Silas were and a few minutes later they emerged with them.

"We must follow them," Alex said, "They are our only hope for Irana."

Quickly, the boys put on their sandals and followed the group of men who were very respectfully escorting Paul and Silas from the prison. Once out of the prison the apostles made their way to Lydia's home and went inside.

"Now what?" Matt asked.

"Well!" Alex scratched his head, "they'll be there for a while. Probably the best thing to do would be to go to the riverside this afternoon and ask Ruth for her help to ask Paul if he will come and heal Irana."

"That sounds the best plan," Matt agreed. "But can we now find something to eat? I'm absolutely starving after the exciting night we've had."

Chapter thirty-four

T he two made their way to the market where they bought some fresh bread and sat on a warm stone by the roadside, eating hungrily. They sat for a while watching some girls balancing large water pots on their heads. "I'm glad I'm not a girl," Matt said.

"Yes. Life is hard for them," Alex agreed, "but not as hard as it is for Irana. Which reminds me," he said getting up, "it's time we went to the temple."

Together they made their way to Aphrodite's temple. A group of worshippers were scattering rose petals at the foot of the steps and the boys looked around for the familiar sight of Irana telling someone's fortune.

But she wasn't there.

"Maybe she's already been here and we've missed her," Alex said doubtfully, "We are a bit late."

"That must be it," Matt said, "She's usually here earlier than this."

They waited until midday and then agreed it would be good to go to the place of prayer early so that they could see Ruth. Secretly, they were both worried but didn't admit it to each other. What if Irana had been taken away?

"Tomorrow we'll come early with Paul," Alex said, "if Ruth can persuade him to come."

When they arrived at the riverside the boys were glad
to see Ruth sitting by herself at the edge of the group.

"We need to talk to you," Alex said to her earnestly.

"Go on," Ruth replied, "I'm listening."

Quickly, Alex poured out their story of how they had
been travelling for so long to try to find his sister and how
finally they had found her here in Philippi. Every now and
then Matt interrupted to correct Alex when he made a
mistake in the story.

"So," Alex finished, "We need you to persuade Paul to
come to the temple to heal Irana."

"Oh dear," Ruth said quietly, "I'm afraid that's not
possible. You see," she went on, "Paul and Silas have
left Philippi. They left quite early this morning and are
already on their way to Thessalonica."

"Oh no!" Matt cried despairingly, "Now Irana will never
be healed."

Alex rubbed his hands over his eyes. "We've searched
and searched and now we've found her we may have lost
her again because she wasn't there today and now Paul
has gone too. Oh Matt, whatever shall we do?"

Matt put his hands on his head as if to stop it from
exploding. "Paul was our only hope," he whispered.

"Now that's where you're wrong," Ruth said, and she
sounded quite cross with them, "Our hope is not in Paul
or Silas. Our hope is in Jesus and he is still with us even
though Paul has gone. Now boys, we need to pray that
Jesus will heal Irana," and without waiting for their reply
she bent her head and prayed.

After a while the prayer ended and Ruth looked up and
smiled at them kindly. "It's hard sometimes," she said

gently, "It's hard to believe that God knows best, but even when things seem to be going wrong, God is still good. Just trust him and all will be well."

Chapter thirty-five

The following morning Alex and Matt waited patiently at the temple for Irana to arrive. But they waited in vain. She was nowhere to be seen. They searched the street leading from the temple where they had seen the woman take her each day but could find no clues there.

As they dejectedly made their way back towards the temple area Matt suddenly stopped in his tracks. "Look over there," he hissed at Alex who looked up quickly. "See that big woman?"

"Oh yes!" Alex answered looking at the woman Matt was pointing at, "It's the woman who's usually with Irana. She looks very annoyed."

"Let's go and see what she's saying." Matt said urgently, but Alex was already moving across the courtyard.

"She's completely vanished," the woman was saying, "I got distracted by those interfering foreigners. I was watching them being dragged off to the magistrates. Good riddance I say. But when I turned round the girl had gone. No, not the slave girl! My girl—Irana. No idea where she went. I think I heard her say "Jesus" before she disappeared. Who's Jesus? Some friend of hers I expect. I've got a feeling that Paul person might have got to her as well as the slave girl. I'll give her such a beating when I find her!"

"Is it possible?" Matt whispered to Alex grabbing hold of his arm, "Could she have been healed too?"

"Of course it's possible!" Alex said, "Oh Matt, I wonder where she's hiding? We must find her before that woman does."

"If she's healed," Matt said, "she'll recognise us, so the best thing we can do is to walk around Philippi, through every street and market place until she sees us!"

After several hours of walking they stopped for a rest. "We've walked round the whole of Philippi," Alex said. "Is there anywhere we haven't been?"

"We've not been to the city gate," Matt replied. "And anyway we should go and check the travellers coming up from Neapolis. Let's go there now."

"Ok," Alex said wearily, "I'll be so glad when my father gets here."

As they came near to the city gate they saw the figure of an old woman, wrapped in her shawl, sitting up against a broken fence just off the road. "Let's ask her if she has seen a girl down here today," Matt suggested.

Together they approached her. "Excuse me," Alex said politely, "have you seen a girl with bright red hair passing by here?"

The woman looked up at the boys and as she did so her shawl slipped from her head to reveal a bright mass of red hair and a thin face alight with joy.

"Irana!" Alex cried.

"It is you!" Matt said, clapping his hands together in sheer joy.

"Alex! Matt! What are you doing here?" Irana exclaimed.

In reply, Alex pulled her to her feet and into his arms. "We've found you at last," was all he could say.

By this time all three had tears running down their faces. Alex reached out and pulled Matt into the circle of their arms and the three of them stood together laughing and crying at the same time.

"I prayed and prayed that someone would come along and help me, but I didn't imagine it would be you!" Irana said through her tears. "Oh I have so much to tell you," she went on, "when I heard that man say 'In the name of Jesus Christ ...' suddenly all the evil inside me disappeared. And now I'm well and I do so want to go home."

"I think your wish is about to come true," Matt said, and his voice sounded thick with emotion. "If I'm not mistaken, that looks like our folk coming through the city gates."

The three watched as they saw the familiar figures of Kostas, Jonas and Gabriel amongst a group of travellers moving through the gates.

"Journey's end," Alex said happily, waving his hands to catch their attention.

But just at that moment they saw the figures of a big man and woman bearing down on them. Irana shrank back behind Alex, "It's them," she whispered, her face draining of colour.

"And dad hasn't seen us," groaned Alex.

Matt pushed Alex and Irana towards a pile of posts left there to repair the fence. "Quick! Hide!" he said, but it was too late.

"There she is, the wicked girl," shouted the big woman.

Helplessly, they watched as the couple came closer. "Dad! Gabriel!" they shouted at the top of their voices to the crowd at the gate some thirty metres away. They waved frantically trying to get their attention but their family were looking in the opposite direction.

"It's no good, they can't hear us with all the people around them talking," Matt said.

He turned to see Alex picking up a long fence post. "That won't do any good," he sighed as the man drew even closer, his hand reaching out to grab Irana who was cowering behind Matt.

But Alex wasn't listening. He was running forward, the fence post held like a javelin in a steady horizontal line. The large man paused in his tracks as Alex ran past him. Then, the post left his hand and sailed into the air. Straight as an arrow it flew and landed at the feet of Gabriel who quickly turned to see where it had come from.

"There they are!" Gabriel shouted and broke into a run.

"Praise God!" cried Jonas as he and Kostas also began to run towards them.

Seeing them coming the man and woman hesitated. They could see they were no match for these three men, as well as the amazing boy who had thrown the fence post equal to any Olympic javelin thrower. Hastily, they turned away and with a curse returned to the path leading back into the city.

The next moment Alex was swept off his feet by his brother, while Jonas hugged Matt and Kostas tenderly held Irana in his arms.

"God does answer prayer," Alex said at last, "He is very great and very good."

Jonas looked up over Matt's head and smiled, "And God can also use two determined boys and a champion javelin thrower to be the answer to our prayers."

DISCOVERING THE HIDDEN LAMB

Gill Jacobs

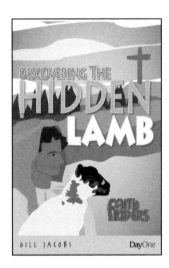

A story of two lambs: the orphaned lamb Ben cares for, and Jesus, the Lamb of God. Bible events woven into this story are seen through Ben's eyes as he struggles to understand who Jesus is while trying to save his pet lamb from being sold for sacrifice at Passover. The reader discovers what life was like in Palestine during Jesus' time, and why the Lamb of God had to die.

Much of Gill Jacobs' working life has been with young people both within the church and as a Paediatric Occupational Therapist. She runs training in special needs for professionals and has also been involved in writing parenting courses. Her husband John is a Messianic Jew. They live in Hampshire and have two grown-up daughters.

Also available

ESCAPE FROM DANGER

Gill Jacobs

Naomi is a young girl living in
Damascus who runs away from home
because of her violent stepfather.

The story traces her many adventures
as she travels to Jerusalem and
struggles to survive alone. The biblical events woven into the story
begin at the cross where 'Discovering the hidden lamb' (Gill
Jacobs' first book) ends. Naomi is caught up in the events in
Jerusalem following the resurrection of Jesus. These events are
seen through Naomi's eyes as she struggles with the theme of
forgiveness. Can she forgive those who have treated her so badly?
This book has been written to help children to understand what
life was like for the early church, and the importance of being
forgiven and of forgiving others.

NEVER GIVE UP ON YOUR DREAMS

Mary Weeks Millard

Gabrielle is six years old when her swimming instructor realizes that she has a natural talent and arranges for her to have extra swimming coaching. Through her dedication and self-discipline, and with the support of her family and especially her granny, Gabrielle gets better and better, and everyone thinks that she will soon be able to compete in the Olympics. She dreams of winning an Olympic gold. But one day, disaster strikes. What will happen to her Olympic dreams now?

Mary Weeks Millard used to work as a missionary in Africa. She now loves to write stories for younger readers.